GHOSTSPEAKING

Several of these poems or prose pieces appeared (sometimes in earlier versions) in the following: *Arc Magazine* (Canada), *Cordite*, *A Festschrift for Tony Fraser* (England), *Mascara Literary Review*, *Meanjin*, *Rabbit*, *Shearsman* (England), *Southerly*, *Text*. "The well" and "I do not trust that word 'oxygen'" appeared in French translation in *Tôt le matin et autres poèmes*, Recours au poème éditeurs, 2015.

First published 2016 by Vagabond Press
PO Box 958 Newtown NSW 2042 Australia
www.vagabondpress.net

Designed and typeset by Michael Brennan.

ISBN 978-1-922181-78-7

PETER BOYLE

GHOSTSPEAKING

VAGABOND PRESS

CONTENTS

FEDERICO SILVA

LAZLO THALASSA (ADDITIONAL TRANSLATIONS)

ANTONIO ALMEIDA

THE MONTAIGNE POET

ROBERT BERECHIT

ANTONIETA VILLANUEVA

ERNESTO RAY

ELENA NAVRONSKAYA BLANCO

(ADDITIONAL TRANSLATION)

GASTON BOUSQUIN

PACKAGE RECEIVED FROM MEXICO CITY, DECEMBER 2015

RICARDO XAVIER BOUSOÑO

(ADDITIONAL TRANSLATION)

No puedo hablar con mi voz sino con mis voces.
                    – Alejandra Pizarnik, "Piedra Fundamental"

I cannot speak with my voice – only with my voices.

Le seul véritable voyage, le seul bain de Jouvence, ce ne serait pas d'aller vers de nouveaux paysages, mais d'avoir d'autres yeux, de voir l'univers avec les yeux d'un autre, de cent autres, de voir les cent univers que chacun d'eux voit, que chacun d'eux est; et cela nous le pouvons avec un Elstir, avec un Vinteuil, avec leurs pareils, nous volons vraiment d'étoiles en étoiles.
                    – Marcel Proust, *La Prisonnière*

The only true journey, the one Fountain of Eternal Youth, isn't travelling to new landscapes, but having other eyes, seeing the universe with the eyes of another, of a hundred others, seeing the hundred universes that each of them sees, that each of them is; and with an Elstir, with a Vinteuil, with those like them, we can do that, we truly can fly from star to star.

RICARDO XAVIER BOUSOÑO
(1953 – 2011)

Ricardo Xavier Bousoño was born in Posadas in Argentina in 1953, the second son of a conservative local lawyer and an impoverished socialite from Buenos Aires. He left Argentina in 1976, fearing for his life as the activities of the military and right-wing death squads intensified. After living in Brazil for twelve years he went to Spain with a long-term lover who found work there as a pianist. His final years were spent in Veracruz, Mexico.

Bousoño was a successful painter and installation artist as well as poet. His two collections of poetry are *Utilities* (1983) and *Chronicles of a Wedding* (1987). He died in Veracruz in 2011.

SELECTED POEMS FROM *UTILITIES* (1983)

HOUSE ARREST IN SÃO PAULO

1.

And while I slept the clouds came in –
these clouds they have here
that occupy cities for a month or for a decade,
that shift slightly at irregular moments,
clouds like deep sleepers
turning in their own imprisoned dreams

so that children climbing a hill in daylight
are at once lost in night,
streetlights come on, birds recognise
familiar purple grass in trimmed
dry patches

and a year of cloud weather moves so quickly,
you age so fast.
The speed with which I write
testifies to the shrinking multiplying
inner sprawl of the universe.
They have lodged me in this high-rise hotel,
official guest of a Writers',
Artists', Ergo-econometricians' Archival
Thought-Fest, downtown São Paulo,
prisoner 25967 in this

bugged lab of babble.
Once the nomads have entered you
there's no way of going back,
no way to slow the chaos in the blood.

2.

Antonio Moneda created the three
rust continents that exist.
On them eyes grow into a bent heaviness,
the spine of the prisoners
is all one spine
so the act of breakage can be
singular and simultaneous.
When at night
a finger wakes in a drawer under the stove
it understands but cannot think through to the end
what a body was.

Say this only:
what happened elsewhere
speaks now because
there is no elsewhere.

I am writing from my space
in this many-layered house inhabited
by slowly dysfunctioning monsters. Wayward
transmission signals set the walls aglow.
Surveillance cameras with bovine faces

burn holes in the fake
stability of floorboards.
They have instructed me to climb into my coffin
and not get out:
an everyday request.
I retorted (mildly I thought) with a list
of instructions for my (twice daily) cocktail.
I have hopes for the gradual
transmigration of my brain.
To eat: wild rocket, salamanders,
soft cheese and silence.

3.

The statue of Christ the birds feed on –
its green moss wets their beaks –
the sky of the underworld
is a trickle of blue sound
from a space below his lips.

Above the roar
of a city roused to its own pain at daybreak
I feel his gaze
walk with me down the darkened halls.
Poor broken clay, so little
to offer, a light-bulb
at the farthest end of a dead-end street,
wired to the sun for a thousand years.

4.

In the Montenegrin heiress's dream of spring
the alchemist has left his crystals
out in the rain. The full moon
has done its worst and passing predators –
the one-eyed motorcyclist, screech owls,
foxes that have lost the art
of metamorphosis –
distrust these cold star-shaped
brightnesses.
A chalice left in a forest
will blossom only as rust.

5.

At this distance, too far
for herbs or auscultation, too close
for exorcism, I circle
a slow dying.
Now in the season of hungry birds
I watch my hand's crimson thread spill out.
The splintering of the back
continues forking.
Inside the sky of the cerebellum
a tiny microbe-spider blows bubbles
on a bent twig of cartilage.

I dreamt I climbed into the bottle
to become a message
and then they drained the sea.

6.

In the month of the great rains,
when my coffin was a ship
on the sidewalks of São Paulo,
navigating between the legs
of fruit-shop girls and secretaries,
I understood
life is explosion.
The night sky and the cries of street vendors
come close.
They whisper, "Now,
it is now you'll see."

7.

The wind is light here, the ocean promised
and everything is distance and becoming.
If I could step outside the window
and stand in air
I would be completely calm in its radiance.
Even the traffic today
is like a distant calligraphy splashed
on the tassels of a temple curtain.

Enter now:
strike the gong with the ritual clapper,
bow three times, shake
the row of paper slips suspended on thin wires,
snatch one blindly to know your fortune.

My coffin opens on the world
and, all around me, the black walls are
dazzling light I haven't learnt to
feel yet. In the slower faster drift of
time-frames other than ours, extra-terrestrial life
falls through us and, almost,
I could be there inside it.
Listen to the creaking of trees
from before the time of the dinosaurs.
On the other paths life spiralled down
you can hear the dizzying journey that explodes
in the thousand-layered symphony
of bird song.

8.

For days now there is no sign of sky.
From the coffin
I watch the mirroring grey swirls –
nothing beyond –
by night the same:
a wall against the stars.
The drinks have long since stopped,

the door is bolted.
Wiry spiders race across my books,
voices from neighbours' TV sets
argue softly in the distance.
Through a broken window
sometimes they lower an apple
or a plate of food scraps.
The world above goes on:
small signs suggest the hope of
an erratic heaven.

9.

He is waving to me
from the farthest room
at the end of innumerable corridors:
the ghost I will become.

Nothing
in the history of the universe
has so tenderly familiar
a face.

10.

A five-pointed word stranded in blankness –
points five simultaneous directions,
a word alone

indicating the loss of direction, the presence
of many directions, the refusal to guide.

I stand by my word,
will not relinquish it, to the death
it tokens me, the bird of haunted night
has flown clear through me
and the lice off its back have entered
the word.

The lice now inhabit the word,
along with the wind, the night,
these paper walls, the thousand
sheets of mirroring glass,
an old man and his faith
in meanings.

AURA OF THE POEM

The poem travels just ahead of the traveller.
It checks in for the night,
lowers the blinds,
makes tea.
The traveller gets angry with the flight delays,
is held up
by missing baggage,
gets soaked to the skin by
the unpredictable downpour of the one
torrential evening of the dry spell.

The poem sits and waits,
warms the room,
arranges all to make it welcoming.
Sometime after midnight
the traveller turns the key
and the glow of some
unfathomable beauty
dries the anguished moisture
on his skin.

FROM A TRAVELLER'S NOTEBOOK

1.

A bridge has been laid down across the abyss
and on it I recognise a figure walking:
diminished and with a piece taken out of the soul
but still myself.
The flowers in my hand are black
but the green water is a voice
that flows by unconcerned.
I listen for the slow sharp ringing of the bell that says
the snow is falling.
In the high mountains the white trees
prepare themselves for spring.

2.

How many suitcases to bring with you
to the house that casts no shadows?
Despite the furious declensions, no one and nothing
in all the corridors of the sky
understands your subtle post-aorist tenses:
your unique way to say
what the past would have chosen
under its heaven of mutated stars and celestial algae.
Know this clearly:
now and for this once only
you are leaving the earth.

3.

The guttering ran the way it had to
along the edges of the sky.
The man is looking at his watch.
The trains in this place are imprecise.
What is this moment to him?
The train door about to open –
the dull shine of posters opposite,
one hand around the grip of a backpack,
the other at his side.
A mountain is growing in the back of his head.
Words fall short of nature
but words fall short of everything.

4.

He stepped past the Guardian Dogs at the temple entrance.
On the wall above him Chinese signs
for enclosed empire, for mountain and river
and the boxed windows of rain.
The growling of griffons off to the left.
At the altar, throwing sacred coins,
he asked for his name and fate.
Incense rose from bowls that drifted
on a lake of rose water.
Last night's dream: a sluggish river clogged with old tyres.
The coins told him only "You have no permission to ask."

5.

I remember the boatman on the high mountain lake:
his cupped hands bearing fire across the water.
So you carry me beside you
on the ferry over black waters.
Beside you, beside your veiled ghost-face,
I am the soul of an old lampshade left out on the kerb,
the resonating heart of the empty biscuit box.
Hold me among the hours of the living.
What sounds still
in the vast surrounding heaven.

GHOSTSPEAKINGS

1.

And you came floating,
a white witch in flowing robes,
dishevelled shirt sleeves, pockets emptied,
trousers dangling and twisted,
a few feet above the ground
between the grey unfolding banners
of the one road through the blind forest.
And I, a ghost led by a ghost
on the white road where autumn is
and the tam-tam drumming of the dead,
the wild sky ablaze with fairy lights to blind us,
the swarming blackberry bush of God,
its voice, a thousand bees,
rises up inside me, this raw-edged
world that leads me,
as always,
to the small scooped
hollow of amazement,
my grave, my swirling
galaxy.

2.

(The mystic ants in the shoe depository)

The blaze of light in lost eyes.
Each black speck expanding
to start once more its uncompleted wanderings,
the shoes with their tongues drooping
to lap the bitter dust.
And the ants shine in a heaven of leatherwork,
frayed and forgotten
drinking in a cosmos.

3.

This is the door through which I enter the world of dawn.
Darkness surrounds it,
darkness makes it – three panels
give it shape,
the emptiness through which I step.
Wider than darkness,
this halo of hammering rain,
flowing criss-crossed speech,
dark water like the currents of my blood,
through you too
I step.

Rain and dawn
and darkness –

you three I know,
you three
release me
to myself.

I DO NOT TRUST THAT WORD "OXYGEN"

1.
In the tent below the sacred mountain
gold banners flutter.
Death hovers over you: a blue lantern,
a grey beginning, so it starts,
cosy (almost) and riveting
as the last word
of the last episode of the Korean serial
"Ripening into sky-flowers."

2.
The stone-Emperor's garden is made of cloth –
so many Emperors, so many gardens,
each with its distinct style, its spiky rules.
Quick, you must find a cloth to offer
at the second altar of the first gate –
trade favours with the merchant's seamstress wife,
she of the macramé lips, and implement
your action plan for falling meteorites.
If the wind is from the west
transform your body into whirlybirds
peeled off the maple tree's stern
countenance. Outlive the carp
in their ferocious flesh-pond.
If you meet the Emperor
it's best to be as invisible

as the first snowflake in an autumn sky.
In these long years of imperial silence
fear is the calligrapher's secret mantra.
All those beautiful lines of flowers
splashed lightly over fields
of hacked bones.
In your ear a terrified twilight climbs.
Know you're on your own.

3.
I went to the mask maker's house,
a single step that lifted me
over the top of the grey mountain.
A room the size of a phone box
with wire meshing to catch the flight of birds,
eyes afloat across windows,
clouds peering in.

The mask maker had died
but the room kept weaving masks,
a galaxy of approaching worlds,
this fear behind my face.

4.
Cousin Morabito holds the flag with the drowned fly.
He signals some kind of future, I interpret:
You don't know what it is to take off,
arms turned to wings, a new sense of space

rippling by against the chest,
trusting as a leaf that takes to the wind
and flexes the immense energy
of earth's spin. Only listen:
the neighbour's basketball thuds
against the cement path to the small
Mayan temple precinct built against the roof.
A great thunder is coming. Leave
before the knives are polished.

5.

The wisteria signature bleeds into the moonlight.
The golden edges of the books
demand a name.
We will have to consult the index to lost things.
We will first assign a number
to each forgotten pin-point of the world,
the fifth rock in the crumbling valley, what the sea
borrows from the inner ear.
All must wait for the great
assigning of names, entrusted to
the cantankerous librarian
in the Ministry for Skimping. While,
just beyond the queue to join the world,
a lotus floats
buoyant in its own
amnesia of the head abbot's last sermon
Fifty-five days in Nirvana.

6.
In the zoo café
my illuminated eyelids skim the foam
of daybreak, lightly stirred.
Pen poised above the blank page,
I am caged with my cappuccino
and feel more than ever at a loss
required (a bequest from the Ministry
of Wastage) to transcribe
my lost years.
The squat komodo dragon
will be here soon on his
afternoon patrol, eating flies off the zinc bar,
devouring foot-loose tourists.
His hazy eyes and flickering tongue
lurch past my cage
on the terrace of the zoo café,
myself, stalled
long-distance lyric sprinter,
sole exhibit.

7.
With a long stick Wittgenstein
writes script on the sand
and the shoveler of cement nods
and indicates an end to becoming.
With the stamp of a hazelnut
on the settling slurry
the tablets of forgetting are forged –

there will be
no memory, no way to return
to life in summer, to the jetty that led
beyond the mangroves.

Whatever,
the man with the sandblaster says
winding up the crank on the oxy-acetylene
for the final burn-off.
From far above
in the sky of all our origins
wingless angels, brown moths,
drop into the soup.

8.
Empires of a breath, forests of a grass-blade:
instructed by the rolling vistas of collapse
search out the minima.
Go down into the neon of the world,
go down into the strange ooze,
rich heart-flesh of turtles,
eyes of the invisible.
They are not for you: whatever has been said,
whatever written.
Come back to life with no left, no right,
no this or that,
tenseless, verbless, stateless,
decidedly no words for "is" or "was,"
no convolutions over "think" and "know."

Let the purity of dawn flood you,
let the single act of a first breath
shatter the cosmos.

9.
Microbes and memory chips usurp the biosphere.
Happy those whose feet go down into the earth –
ah, the whispers of necrophiliac spring,
faint sounds of bells suspended
in the ears of new-born calves,
ancient rituals to heal brain-madness.
Here only
a brittle cannibalistic sanity reigns.
Expendable,
each stamped with our own discard-by date,
we gaze into the lure of the great devouring.
Pears and oranges have migrated to still-lifes
buried in a recluse millionaire's sealed vault.
We have unlearned the compass:
so there might be
no signs to read, no way to follow.
Meanwhile, close by,
almost scraping our heads, they are adjusting
the valves in those pink-glowing canisters.
I do not trust that word: "oxygen."

FROM *CHRONICLES OF A WEDDING* (1987)

FREIHEIT

Wherever you live you can find them,
Prussian outposts:
In the fork of a tree
the leopard's head with his tongue
trailing down. In a suburb with no name
a twist of wire from the underworld and,
sunk in its garden of criss-crossed trenches,
the house of the mandrake roots.
Just by breathing and accidentally
opening your eyes you see them,
Prussian outposts. It's no good saying
the fish from the Royal Pond perished
years ago of frost-bite or the same
mysterious starvation as
the local tribes. The vast repertoire
of the northern sun of arctic darkness
always begins afresh right here. This day.
Mixed with the tar of your hometown street
and the tang of an open sewer
drink it down, this elixir
exploding in your head like a light-bulb in
a backroom where the all-night TV
transmits football and a thousand

small losses, each one stamped with your name
and all fatal,
murga durga, kali candomblé unglückliche
Freiheit, das macht nichts.

AN ORDINARY DAY IN UZBEKISTAN

The fruit grower climbs out of the sky
as the butcher of day-old lambs
wipes the blood from his apron.
"Ah, your strawberries smell of cold mist
and the drool of anaemic angels flows in your veins."
They were building Babel off to the left
as the polyglots sharpened their skills
round the chessboard.
All over the city with its high-rise anxiety
the whisper ran of the impending coup.
From the land of milk and honey
my parents arrived: mother leading father by the hand,
father with his pure gold walking stick
making Masonic signs in the air.
"There's a full tank in the Cadillac. You're no Uzbecki –
we're here to get you out. Within hours
the generalissimo will have the roads sealed off,
then the planes will come in laden with sarin gas.
He's got plans for this country and people aren't part of it."
My friends crowd me out, eyes pleading
like bobbing balloons of trust
in the portholes of the Titanic.
How can I abandon the salt of the earth,
the cousins of the fruit grower and his prolific
multiply-incestuous family?
Next thing my parents are gone,
stripped from the sky

like news headlines in this tropic downpour.
A siren sounds: we're all trying to get out now,
the fruit growers, impressed peons from the Babel work-gang
and a bunch of bearded poets,
dodging our way through the forest.
While the generalissimo's planes roar by overhead
and in the distance bombs drift down.
There is no hijacking in this poem
though a small band of war-painted types in mufti,
clandestine connoisseurs of torture,
are tiptoeing across the edges of the poem
to remind me they could at any moment
gatecrash this kingdom of words.

A day like any other in Uzbekistan.
The normality project going on in one corner
and the loading of sarin canisters in another.
The generalissimo's effigy
imprints itself on a forest clearing,
his gaunt face a patchwork of tiny stickers
marked "Order" and "Cleansing of parasites."
Babel always there to be renewed,
one more development fiasco
in the land of glib.

RICARDO XAVIER BOUSOÑO: AN INTERVIEW

Ricardo Xavier Bousoño greeted me with a broad smile at the door to his small apartment on the outskirts of Veracruz. It was my first trip to Mexico and I was finding it hard coping with the crowds and the noise and the sheer difficulty of travelling in the relentless heat. Soon I was comfortably seated under the air conditioning and, with Ricardo's permission, had set the small recorder going for our interview. In all, during my week in Veracruz, we met three times for a long afternoon chat, so what I reproduce here is, in fact, an edited version of three interviews.

A recurrent theme of Ricardo's conversations was his sense of being passed over, never mentioned in awards, not invited (or, worse, deliberately uninvited) to festivals, excluded from magazines, having to fund the publication of his own books. Without the modest success of his paintings and installations he would have starved long ago, he confessed. "My trouble was I'm an apolitical poet – at least in the sense people understood things in the 70s and 80s. I'm gay. I would have been dead if I'd stayed in Argentina. I hate the fascist bastards but I was never about to fall in love with Fidel. Always my instinct has been not to trust idealist programmes, not to trust any group that promises salvation. I had the misfortune of being a 21st Century poet stranded in the 20th Century. I was born sceptical, some would say cynical but I don't use that word. No one wanted to publish me. I wasn't part of the in-group. I once had a dream I met Neruda and he told me I had a bad smell. Or maybe it was a bad spell. It was a crazy dream, all in English. I once met Marquez in Caracas and said to him, 'If you think Fidel's so great would you want a Communist dictatorship for Colombia?' 'No, not for Colombia,' he said, 'It wouldn't work there.' 'Listen,' I said, 'you motherfucker, so it's all right for Cuba to be fucked over by Castro and his cronies but not Colombia. You know in Cuba they'd lock me up too and probably torture me for good measure just for the hell of it. I don't trust any dictatorship.'"

When I met Ricardo that afternoon in late August 2010 he was already very sick. At fifty-seven he looked like a man in his nineties. He told me it wasn't the drugs he'd done all those years – it was cancer. He was already in the final stages of bone cancer. I offered to go away and stop bugging him. "No, no," he insisted. "I'm curious to have someone from so far away interested in my work. If you want to translate my poems that's fine. Though in a way oblivion would be better."

I asked about Brazil where he spent seven years after getting out of Argentina in 1976. "Weird," he said, "Gullar escaped Brazil to be safe in Argentina and I escaped Argentina to be safe in Brazil. Back then there were monsters everywhere. You just had to get lucky – I was lucky. You've seen our dear friend Fernando – you know what they did to him?" I knew. I didn't have to be told. I'd seen the burn scars on his arms and legs. Thirty-five years later. While through a haze his hand and eyes had indicated his whole body. And then he'd described how they did it. "I didn't want to write political poems," Ricardo went on, "I didn't want those bastards to think they'd captured my psyche for the rest of my life. I didn't want to give them that satisfaction. But everyone's different. I respect deeply, very deeply," he added, making sure I'd caught the seriousness of his voice, "those like Cardenal or Raúl Zurita who live and write out of their commitment, out of their need to speak of horrors. And I respect Juan Gelman of course, there's no need to say it, for all he does, though seventy percent of his poetry is I think pretty slight, one-dimensional or very thin you could say, but that's not the point. I can only be myself. I tried at first in the late seventies but I could never sit down and write poems of witness. Partly because of my temperament. Partly because they never got me and it would feel like bad faith to write poems about comrades or the whole Neruda shit. I got lucky: I escaped in time. So how can I pretend to some kind of martyrdom? When I first got to Brazil I wanted to write political poems. For the first three years in São Paulo, one hour, two hours early morning every day I tried to write. Nothing, blank, nada. The rest of the day I painted – that worked. Then one day, I had my own place by then, I sat there as usual and it just came to me, the whole nightmare of my first six months in São Paulo. Cooped up in a friend's apartment, afraid of my own shadow, can you imagine it? 'Don't go out,' he'd say all the time, 'You can't trust anyone. There's police informants everywhere and they'll sell you to the secret police just to get the money for a bus trip to visit their sick mother in the countryside.' I used to joke with him that I was under house arrest – so that's when I wrote the poem you've translated 'House Arrest in São Paulo' – that was the first poem in my book *Utilities*. I remember writing it very rapidly in two days back in December 1979."

Bousoño's living room was lined with books in several languages – French, German, English, as well as Spanish.

Just as in Eugenio Montejo's Caracas apartment that I visited in 2005, there was an LP of Alec Guiness reading *The Waste Land*. Bousoño explained how Latin American poetry had always been cutting edge and eclectic. It wasn't something invented in the 1980s by the neo-baroque poets. "Vallejo published *Trilce* in 1922 and it's more avant-garde, more out there, than anything written in Europe at the time," he went on, "whereas, from what I've read, Australian poetry didn't enter the 20th Century till the 1970s with Forbes and Tranter." I wanted to protest that this was unfair to poets like Webb, Slessor and Brennan but I didn't want to interrupt the forward rush of his ideas. In any case, in a way he was right.

I asked him about *Chronicles of a Wedding* and whether Perlongher's *Austria-Hungría* was an influence there. "Of course I knew Perlongher," he replied, "but our poems are quite different. I was never as political and I wasn't into Santo Daime. He didn't invent the comparison of the Argentine military with the Nazis either – many of them saw themselves as the Nazis and said so, often. But that poem 'Freiheit,' it says 'Wherever you live you can find them' and that's what I meant. It's not just Argentina. It's a global thing. Look at your country. It's more obvious now, but even in the 1970s you had your own CIA coup when the socialist Whitlam was toppled. And I gather you're building your own Guantánamo at Port Hedland or Nauru, incarcerating refugees, asylum seekers and illegals. The script is set and the client states follow. As someone wrote a few years ago in the New York Times, 'We are all torturers now.'" The conversation stopped, and the room suddenly narrowed and darkened as his words sank in.

I asked how he got to Brazil and how he came to know Ferreira Gullar. "There's a strange story in that," he said. "About a month before the coup a friend tipped me off how they planned to kill every gay in Misiones – he said this was not a joke, systematically they planned to do this and maybe starting within a week. So I caught the bus to Bernardo de Irigoyen and then walked over the border. There were so many people on the road and I had papers from a friend of a friend in the Gendarmerie so I could get out. There were hundreds of people leaving like that – on buses, walking, by private car, whatever. So I was walking towards a bus station in the first big town after the border. I looked around and there, standing right next to me on a street corner, was this guy I recognised from my home town, an elderly guy, 'the one true inhabitant of Misiones,' that was what everyone called him. All his life he was writing this book. Whenever you met him he had it with him: vast printed sheets he'd sometimes wrap round him in folds like a flag, or tuck under one arm so he looked like he was carrying a boat. He filled small square-lined exercise books with his poems, all written with his favourite fountain pens in blue ink, and every year or so he'd take them to a friend who had a small printery. That's how he made his famous 'Editions of one.' 'It's a true book,' he'd say, 'it doesn't dissolve in the rain.' Somehow we all guessed it was a single long poem tracing the true story of an imagined place, maybe in Argentina or Brazil or Paraguay. I asked him what he would do now the great evil had come. He said somewhere, not too far across the border, he'd wait it out, wait till the monsters had gone. I said it would be a long wait. He said nothing to that, just looked beyond me into the trees and the darkening sky. I've thought about him and his book for a long time now. I've never read it – never even skimmed part of it. He didn't let people read it. I asked him once but he said I wasn't ready yet. Never 'it' wasn't ready – just me. That's how he always was."

Later Ricardo talked a little about his friendship with Ferreira Gullar and all his years in Brazil. "It's funny. After *Utilities* and *Chronicles of a Wedding* I virtually stopped writing for decades. And then, five years ago, I started again. Over the past five years I've been writing something new, very short. Completely unlike the poems you've been translating – those were all from the 80s. I've been going backwards, wanting to write something simple, narratival, almost like the Beats, a little like Gullar's *Poema Sujo* maybe, though not really. I'm too close to death for bitterness or cynicism or being clever. I've used up all my irony." He went back into his bedroom and brought out a folder, a *carpeta*, with a string binder and a sheaf of pages with short narrow poems on them. "Take these," he said. "But don't mix them with the other ones. If you want to publish them put them in a separate section. You can leave out my name if you like. Just leave people guessing. Remember: these ones I want to be simple."

I still remember his final words to me at the doorway as I left. "I was lucky – that's all. Inside myself I'm a coward and I don't think my existence or non-existence is a big deal. Tomorrow, next month, next year, I'll vanish like mist."[1]

---

1 The article Bousoño refers to is by Mark Danner, *New York Times*, January 6, 2005.

ELENA NAVRONSKAYA BLANCO
(1929 – 2014)

Elena Navronskaya Blanco (1929-2014), Argentine novelist and poet, is the author of eight novels, three collections of short fictions and four collections of poetry. Born into a family of minor landowners of mixed Russian and Spanish origins in the province of Rosario, Navronskaya Blanco achieved immediate national recognition with the publication of her first novel in 1968 *Nadie olvidará ese desayuno tranquilo al centro del huracán* (*No one will forget that calm breakfast at the centre of the hurricane*). After the death of her husband in 1970 she supported herself and her three children through her work as a school teacher as well as the income from her writing. *Un calendario exquisito para enviar al Duque de la Locura* (Ateo Editores, Buenos Aires, 2004) is her most recent poetry collection.

In our brief correspondence, courtesy of her Buenos Aires publisher, Elena writes {my translation}: "I am of course willing to help clarify the odd phrase or the occasional Argentinismo in standard Spanish – as you know, I have virtually no English. Maria {the publisher} will have no doubt told you I don't do interviews or personal revelation. I am neither an actress nor a politician and, accordingly, detest biographies. The poems should stand on their own."

POSTSCRIPT

Several years after translating a sample of "An Exquisite Calendar for the Duke of Madness" I came across Navronskaya Blanco's 1996 book *Los Muertos*. The reader will find a translated excerpt later in this anthology.

AN EXQUISITE CALENDAR FOR THE DUKE OF MADNESS

A simple flat bottomed boat was the most practical vehicle to travel across to that other shore with its tightly bordered countries, its languages and customs jostling so close against each other, one nation's bed sheets poking into the eyes of another's laundry, shelves crammed with receptacles for all flying and crawling beings. She had wandered into a land that was called madness. It exploded outwards in her dreams – the cast too heavy, too many people crowding into narrow corridors, massed outside on the landing, the floorboards bound to give way. She was dressed like Ophelia, like a jester garlanded in marigolds. At the same time destiny had singled her out to be a Renaissance prince, fumbling with numerous cards all inscribed with the names of flowers, waiting nonchalantly for the beheading.

And then she was there suddenly far ahead of me – on the small road that leads into the heart of the sky. And I was stuck where I was, here amid the wild silence of dead voices.

* * *

Among the colours making up the house was the red brown of blood issuing from every pore of her skin. The open window with the chill breeze coming in served only to dry the brownish lines, an inner unstoppable calligraphy. Rain, as it trickled in, added a blue wash to everything and, late at night, the stars carved icy pinpoints of silver. All day green fronds, wisteria, tiger lilies, purple buddleia and the most waterlogged hydrangeas cast their shadows on the walls. Even at midnight she could feel them multiplying like a swarm of black butterflies. In the cold of 2 a.m. the rain had finally lulled the frogs to sleep.

Meanwhile those stranded some distance from their bones made enquiries on their cell phones and an old man dropped by to tune a harpsichord that had sheltered from the monsoon in the basement. And she knew any moment she would meet the small girl with the damaged legs who had learned to fly and the armless painter with bottomless eyes and no nose. When a true witch throws the yarrow-stalks of the dream, the sleeper will travel immense distances and wake convinced the myriad chances of life form a single path.

* * *

Within days the trees arrive. The litany of warriors finishes. The roll call of decapitations reaches an end. While in the mountains winter is laying out its precious dust that tastes of arsenic, it is summer still among the loquat trees by the lake. Once, when strange voices screamed and wept and shattered the house, the three of us children slipped away to the field by the river to tell each other stories and sleep. On the second night as we camped there suddenly the sky was no longer visible. Benign, withered and made entirely from the hair of old dolls, a forest had settled over us. The small boy with the long white shirt who sleeps under my eyelids woke up then. As if to calm himself, his lips were softly intoning: "In another lifetime I will be here among you, straight as a tree, alive and simply blossoming."

* * *

After the rains came the season of rats, of blood red thistles and boundless peaches, the sudden growth of fingernails, of fields laced with blue skies and immense plains that metamorphosed into storks. Those were the curiously curved afternoons when families deciphered codices in the cool of the orchard and when black swallows visited from their kingdom of midnight under the earth. Beauty stood, a naked replica scratched to pieces by the claws of willful cats, and the gallery of abstractions had to be draped and stored away in the vaults of abandoned small-town banks at the edge of the lonely wheat fields. For this season was the harbinger of immense space and the precision of sudden arrivals, preposterous combinations of numbers and scribbled lines, ingredients and beings rising out of soil. How alert everyone was. Sleep was unheard of in those days. Sunlight unfolded, as did the quaint maps left by dead promises, numerous designs for impossible machines, the at-last-revealed instructions for a world so absurd the whole family could only break up laughing, then send a runner out for more wine. In those days hands opened, enmities were forgotten, the black shirt and suit of mourning ripped spontaneously apart, and so grandfather, tottering on the balcony with his cigar, would survey how the distances suddenly stood open and pronounce, "Today for fifteen minutes there is no more death."

* * *

And at once we entered that moment of the year when for days winter blossoms inside the raging heat of summer. "Snow falling into bushfires" some call it, others "the divided air". The Antarctic zone has begun its migration across the pampas while circling tropic storms seek to bring life back to the lost cities of the southern pole. All creatures are confused. Now is the time when harvesters bring in crops of blighted misfortune. The soil is cleared in readiness for the sowing of interstellar particles. Minerals never known before wash up on beaches. This is not a time for marriage, for giving birth or for the auspicious naming of children, animals or plants. Of this season is it written, "Let windows be sealed, let doors stay closed."

* * *

I saw her there, sitting on the narrow ledge outside the window of the upstairs bedroom, my other sister, so pale and thin, the bones almost puncturing her skin. I could tell she was getting ready to fly, that slight rocking of her body, her closed eyes feeling their way towards the air she wanted to float in like someone terrified of water reciting a mantra before slipping off the side of the pool into that blue wide expanse. My other unnamed sister, my lost double, in the thirteenth year of her death.

For many months one year we lived in the capital. I remember the sculptured layers of a park that by gradual degrees raised itself above a boulevard, stretching away from a harbourside marina. The pavements were like Paris or New York with many tall buildings from the 1920s and 1900s, but it was as if someone had taken a huge mallet to every pavement and building and pounded cracks into them. It looked like a New York or Paris systematically dinted so everyone would know it had only ever been a replica, of no real value in itself. People dressed in warm rich clothes and paraded *en famille* along these shattered sidewalks, somehow not taking in that everything was dust and weeds and gaping holes. Everywhere was plastered in billboards of ski resorts, exotic waterfalls, extravagant furs and jewelry, and in the fountain at the centre of the park was a small flotilla of coffins. Around a monument were men dressed like soldiers from the revolutionary war of the 1780s and on the hillside children attached to kites would take off into the skies. I remember there was a small hotel where we stayed one night – when I fell asleep it was on one side of the boulevard and, when I woke the next morning, it was on the other side. There was a yacht owned by the British royal family tied to a tumbledown wharf and, if you walked across the gangplank, you entered another country.

We were living in a place where the past was so strong the present could never really take hold. There was a bookshop that had no books, that had shelves and bookcases lined with names written on small cards indicating where books had once been. There was a museum of the famous leaders and writers and poets and artists of the country but it consisted only of plaques where their manuscripts or paintings or sculptures had once been. In the district of painted buildings there was an immense spiral staircase made of ornately carved ironwork that went down through all the layers of a building that was no longer there. On one street corner a woman who could read fortunes was collecting money so that one day she could buy a Tarot pack. All these things were true of this city, along with the absolute conviction among its inhabitants that nowhere else on earth could match its brilliance or in any way equal its accomplishments. When the last of his business ventures failed, my father hurried us back to our place in the remote provinces.

*   *   *

When I look into the face of the clear ones I look into the face of the sky. Tonight an indistinct lightning is there, like the barely perceptible quivering of a wounded eye. Slowly it circles the platform where I am sleeping driven out of the house by midsummer heat. This is the season of exposure and withdrawal. Simultaneously what is given is concealed. A wave breaks and travels far into the future, into eons when humans are no longer here. The ear picks up a faint crumbling at the edge of perception. You leave the balcony, turn left, up the stairs, waiting for someone to arrive, above the door an oval mirror, then at once you are a blaze of space.

*   *   *

Curled up on the floor a brown leaf that is really a moth –
a moth returning to its state as wood that one day would
return to its state as stone. Soon the table would rise off the
balcony and the small room of light would be inscribed in
the darkness a little way above the forest. Something had
gone wrong, that was all I knew. Faces detached themselves
from other faces. My fearful double chin was dripping blood:
first small droplets, then a steady river flowing down to soak
a tribe of ants on the floor. The twin shadows I knew by the
names of guilt and regret were sitting in opposite corners of
the room, their closed eyes seeing everything.

* * *

What the field before me held were various bells sounding
at different pitches. They hung from the edges of leaves.
A leaf would convulse then stop and somewhere, some
distance from the first leaf, a second leaf would convulse.
This happened for several minutes across the overgrown
orchard with its tangled hedge. The leaves were infected by
some kind of nervous tic, a spasming they could no longer
control, but it was not general, not all the leaves. They
preserved a randomness that made it clear they were just
like us, feeling themselves to be individuals yet dominated
by inexplicable compulsions.

* * *

On a day missing from the calendar there is an hour when
breathing stops, when the breath is no longer needed but every

person will continue across this hour, unaware of its passage. Ants, butterflies, moths and various insects observe people and tamed animals in this hour moving doggedly on with no breath inhaled. It is a moment ordained for every other life form to experience the free creativity of uninterpreted speech. Ants vibrate, worms and caterpillars intone subtle melodies, cockroaches lay bare their dark philosophy. On this day that slips away from human calendars the mosquito and the wasp frame their own elaborate histories. Later humans will breathe in again, unaware of the hiatus, will again insist on their uniqueness, their interminable chant of naming and possessing. In the corner where no light penetrates, the book of beginnings has gained another page.

* * *

One day my father and mother took us to a wedding in a distant city. For two days we travelled by train to reach there, having to change between different lines several times. The wedding took place in the main cathedral and later the reception was held in an old colonial house in a steep and jagged part of the city nestled high in the cordillera known as "the Cinnamon Zone." The house was built round a central patio, an ornate garden with a pond and fountain. The library contained not only the works of the great poets and novelists of many languages but also a sound archive of recordings of every poet who had passed through our country and whose fame or agreed-on merit was considered worth preserving. Surreptitiously I slipped away from my family to rest inside this library. After a while a small woman emerged from under a writing table and identified herself as "the witch" – she could tell fortunes and read off the secret poems inscribed in the palm of the hands or on the surfaces of all old and time-creased objects. These powers, or "toxic gifts" as she called them, had come to her, she told me, in the months after her son had disappeared – her husband was related to a powerful crime lord and someone had stolen her son as revenge for the murder of their family. "This wedding is doomed," she said. "She will beg the Pope to excommunicate her husband and annul the marriage but the President of the Republic is a master of black arts and will blind the church to the truth." I asked her if she knew my fate. "It is not good to know," she replied, "it is never good to know. The time when it will be time is always not that far."

* * *

A season that would last many years was preparing itself. There were people under the floorboards who were growing wolves' teeth and learning to fly in the dark caverns that stretch beneath our country. Those with the precise eyesight for dividing the human body into gristle and sellable commodities. Adept connoisseurs in the pillaging of corpses. Their righteousness would take many years to reach its zenith. It was to be a time with no moon or sun when dismemberment would go on openly, boastingly, for more than a decade. Already under the floorboards they were assembling the racks.

Surely father could hear this and was taking steps. Surely mother could hear it and had alerted someone. Frozen, I listened. Frozen, I held it tight inside myself. It was the shadow of a smile in the rust-green pond I was walking down into. It was a distant ringing in the small curve of my belly, a miniature alarm clock I had no words for, the whispering of a nightmare even before sleep has enfolded you.

*　*　*

They were racing to fortify the borders though no one knew what to put in, what to leave out. Should this tree be in or out? This river, this tangled passionfruit vine? Just as unclear was where to place the barriers of time – only what belonged to last year or twenty years back or a hundred? Should parents be included or only older brothers and sisters? Outside the borders would be everything we would have to abandon and agree to call "enemy" – clipped fingernails, toys from Christmases that couldn't be imitated any more, doubles of ourselves we had chatted to so many times in vivid, impossibly complicated, waking dreams, a friendly shoulder bouncing a ball in a park that had towered over the most difficult year of childhood, a presence that with every casual flick of the expert wrist said, "One day you can be me." And now frantically we were hunting for cardboard boxes, balls of string, spiked wire, the hoarded stash of dumdum shells, swirling laser images of crucified men and women that could stand guard over the frontier, could set the barrier, for once and all, between what we would be from now on and what would be pushed aside into the never more to be mentioned non-land of loss.

* * *

At the conference in the provincial capital each speaker was invited to give their opinions on snow. Voices shifted in a room while enormous clusters of ice crashed against the pavement outside. The city of smashed windows began to spill an almost invisible red thread. The daze in the eyes of a man going blind snowed over and the quiet world waited. In one breath he was standing at the centre of a new unexpectedly luminous world.

White lines flicker like wasps buzzing all around the threaded knots of a grape vine. Petals of whiteness float down around him. Let him die outdoors. And another butterfly settles on his eyelids – from one ear faintly now he hears the purr and slash of an earthmover tearing up the soil, uprooting the trees that held life together. In the other ear a garden fountain goes on letting water trickle down a slope of rocks – water landing in droplets on water. The sudden brightness of snow falling inside him. Before him the wasp doing acrobatics, tumbling from leaf to leaf on the vine. Even with the explosions from the neighbouring yard, the thud of subterranean shelves collapsing, he felt the snow guiding him, the reversal of white and black bringing him to the entrance, this narrow, infinitely open present.

* * *

And Solomon in his whirlwind said

You were a flowering tree.
You were broken donkey and stricken wolf.
You were the one awaited and the one lost.
You were Adam and the one torn to shreds by beasts.
You were the brick and the entire gleaming wall rinsed in
    daybreak.
You were atoms of air and a dream held between bones.
You were the ship.
You were the child who says 'the ship.'
You were the selfish one and the sustainer.
You were the page, the empty whiteness, the dizziness of
    swarming words.
You were the eyes of a frog repeating itself all through the
    long wet night.
You were the lover, the blind man and the grave where
    flowers will grow.
You were raven and owl, the white carcass of a mouse under
    the scrabble of branches.
You were the plum tree and the fly.
You were the stone in the road, the space where the breath
    leaves.
You were Angela and Adam and the voice in the trees where
    the rain falls all night.
You were giver and given, poison and gift.
You were signs in the sky of the ending and someone's hope.
You listened.
You failed.
You were.

* * *

Who comes through the forest?

The bear whose eyes guide him,
who moves in the echoing dark.
The shadow that moves behind him,
the lightning flash that steals the soul.

* * *

In the season of invasions it is not only the mice and spiders
and wasps settling into the hallway. Dark pain moves into
the chest, the skid of twenty years regret slips in through
the soles of the feet. Soldiers of unknown countries take
up positions on the street corners and you can't always be
invisible. This is the cold season when mist comes in off
the sea and damp creeps under your fingernails. You can see
children pressing bread to their faces to stay warm. Worst of
all are the anger plants sending up twisted creepers through
the soil, through the foundations of houses and countless
pinpoints on the body's skin to produce that dizzy nausea
of destructiveness, wild barbs flung at children and partners.
Of this season they say, "Everyone carries a torturer within
them."

* * *

The rain steadily went on falling into itself: gathering like
the round husks of lemons and, when light settled on the

tiles, so much fullness brimmed over my eyes hurt with the shimmer. Pink and red and violet flowers snarled or whimpered or dozed with brief twitches under the assault of rain. It happened in the two weeks before what should have been the pepper harvest, this season they call "death through abundance."

* * *

The whiteness of trees just before sunset with late birds scattering in noisy batches, parrots, Indian mynahs, a raven, some magpies and, come far too early, imposingly out of place as it perches on a low branch in a neighbour's yard, a powerful owl, the Duke of owls, holding the world in its gaze with no flicker of movement, no sound. And darkness grows around it, the bougainvillea gathers a deeper red, night seems to emanate from the leaves and flowers and the black earth, keeping the stars at bay.

The Duke of owls with two misshapen eyes, a card player who owns all the decks, gazing into the emptiness of chance.

* * *

All at once
I come into the wood of the tree,
under flaking bark
the white core of hardness
where everything soars into a flash of eyes

lifted up by light,
ripped to where leaves are hanging in blue greyness
and wind and sky
set everything trembling.

Beyond all terror
I am scattered among fieldmice,
exploded like dewdrops
on leaf mulch, stone and sawn-off tree stump.
And around me
the voices that half whisper,
half chant, "Little sister,
daughter of the daughters of our murderers,
welcome:
our million ghosts,
your million ghosts,
are all here, right here,
breath of the wind inside you.
No one altogether dies."

* * *

In moonlight tainted by clouds something exquisite
shimmers – a broken tin fence, a haze of whiteness?

Midnight on all the drowned clocks. From inside its cold
halo an owl beckons: home.

LAZLO THALASSA (1940 ? – ?)

LAZLO THALASSA: A BIOGRAPHICAL NOTE

This eccentric Mexican poet of mixed Bulgarian and Turkish origins is a shadowy figure whose very existence has been much debated. Lazlo Thalassa's monumental poetic work *Of Fate and Other Inconveniences* is apparently a translation into Spanish of a manuscript found in a small monastery outside Skopje. Though written in Cyrillic script, the original text was long known to be in a non-Slavic language – at first it was thought to be a variant of Greek, Latin or medieval Tuscan but that hypothesis was soon abandoned. After prolonged study Lazlo decoded it as an abandoned off-shoot of old Persian.

Lazlo first contacted me via email with a request that I translate his book from its original Spanish into English. He explained the work as itself a free translation (rather in the manner of Pound's Propertius) of the 15th century poet Hieronymus Gesualdo, a heretic refugee from Urbino who settled on the shores of Lake Ohrid to write his epic in old Persian, a wily stratagem to maximize confusion and escape inquisitorial scrutiny.

In attempting to recreate the shifting mood and deceptive structure of Lazlo's *Of Fate and Other Inconveniences* I imagined it as an expression of Gesualdo's Lake Ohrid, a surface of great sunlight, of pleasure boats and laughter, of holidaying Polish and Russian girls in sultry bikinis with a taste for strong drinks, and beneath it all a river is flowing, a river in the depths of the lake that comes from somewhere higher up and will travel much further, bearing the cold weight of earth's sunless core, to join the oceans of the world. As much a sea as a lake, with storms and unknown dark currents, it is, like that other deep rift of prehistoric water Lake Tanganyika, a trace of something far older than humans, a place that suggests the before and after of a species as much as any private vulnerability.

A final warning to the reader: Thalassa clearly omitted whole passages from the original where he was unable to make sense of Gesualdo's idiosyncratic use of a hieratic language intended to have only one speaker: the King of Kings interceding for his people with the gods. Those who live by the razor perish by the razor. Thalassa's own Spanish was in many places beyond me – words and expressions not in any dictionary, not appearing anywhere on the Web. Several passages he apparently wrote in the dialect of the neighbourhood he grew up in, a barrio of a small town on an island that sank into the southern Caribbean fifty-five years ago. No Spanish speaker I spoke to understood these phrases. I have had to use my own discretion.

POSTSCRIPT

Some time after my work on a version of *Of Fate and Other Inconveniences* Thalassa contacted me again, insisting on his personal reality while admitting that he himself (but fate as well) had been the author of much confusion. He published his poetry under the pseudonym of Lazlo Thalassa, he explained, in part to preserve his anonymity as Miguel Todorov, a research scientist in plate tectonic theory, but mostly to avoid the inevitable confusion with his unrelated namesake Tzvetan Todorov. He wanted to send me a copy of his latest book *El Señor L'Amoroso and Other Strangers* which he thought I might be interested in translating. I soon spotted the stylistic similarities, the love of the Renaissance and the referencing of English literature of the Elizabethan and medieval periods. In *Of Fate and Other Inconveniences* Thalassa references Shakespeare, in the poem I have translated from *El Señor L'Amoroso* it is Malory. There is the same disregard for historic periods and the catapulting of the self into the story. Where else but in Lazlo Thalassa would Dostoyevski brazenly usurp a line of Ezra Pound's? I look forward to translating more of these poems.

LATER ADDITIONAL NOTE

To give the reader greater variety as they read through, I have placed the few translations I have made from *El Señor L'Amoroso and Other Strangers* later in this anthology.

OF FATE AND OTHER INCONVENIENCES

1. (*The fellow travellers of good fortune reach the river of darkness. A very bald fascist lights up a cubicle on the moon. No excuses, no message left.*)

If it was true the Earth had crossed that thin margin where it might continue – its systems breaking down, its oceans' plastic graveyards and garbage mounds gone septic, spawning new poisons in a million eyes and stomachs – how many would be tempted to mass-suicide or mass-slaughter? What new ideologies would arise urging the elimination of some new category of people – the tribe of the Sinestri who dwell in odd-numbered houses, those who say "Da" or "Sí", those who lisp, those who can count beyond 23, those with the wrong genes for heartfelt submission?

2. (*Catholicism plunges 20 points – Buddhist stock holds firm. All this despite continued reports of major attack on the nirvana pipeline by unknown rebel forces in the south. No action recommended.*)

No one knew better how to entertain termites.
From the entrée of her wooden cane
to the after dinner mulch of banana leaves,
grandiose beyond telling,
she was a cynosure for all
winged or crawling creatures, an implacable
outsider to human obsessions,
an old lady seated comfortably in the rain.

3. (*To be or not to be. Wild nights in the cemetery. Cinqueterra ponders.*)

They had led us to a circular swamp or low lake. There they issued us with toothpicks and told us to scour the brackish water for Russians. In a flash I saw our future: we were to be rows of hacked corpses piled each on the other, there in a dry lakebed under the tortured blue sky of paradise.

4. (*Descartes offers analysis. Plotinus a quiet evening with angels. But your shopping trolley is already full with small wedge-shaped cones that all carry the stamp 'made in reality'.*)

Bicycle bells sound and resound along the narrow paths a few moments before sunset. Suddenly the pink has been withdrawn from the sky which has grown merely dark, layered in sea-blue clouds. Orange leaves have fallen all around me. The liner I had been watching all afternoon is no longer there. Precocious geckos are already laying out their geography of night.

5. (*A cigarette twisted on a spike, cones of purple rice, candies in wrappers: such are the offerings for the spirits of the Old People. Again the sea had retreated to reveal its stepping-stones etched with their green inscriptions, the ancient trans-ocean highway.*)

In fifteen seconds all the world's computers entered oblivion.
Born Again Finance Salvationists
fell asleep at their desks,
the death-as-interactive-spectacle project

stranded once more
on some Mesozoic mud bank.
The sea spelt out every name
such as it was in the first noösphere.
Prospero's wand hung suspended
over the frozen dumb show of buffoons and frauds
and each man saw himself
such as he was.

Nymph sheltering in the forest glade
while the motorized cavalcade of zombies passes,
long may the green waters of the world
cover thy nakedness.

6. (*Goalkeeper sent off in thermonuclear meltdown. Lies, lies, scream the punters. No playing field, no winner, rules urban warfare tribunal.*)

On days interrupted by devil worshipping strangers, trying to find in ourselves a ragged ounce of their gentleness, their capacity to let the world be. A sprig of jasmine indicates the contours of the air down which the first mosquitoes of midday, explorers of all standing water, are tracing their tentative map. Elsewhere my lover walks, a canvas hat tilted loosely on her head, her kimono fluttering loose. Damage generates the finest gradations of longing.

7. (*A spider's web inlaid with poisonous stars, shards of glass and old nails. Such is my home, a mansion for security-conscious microbes.*)

We will pluck all the gold vestments from the skeleton. He moves slowly forward with the walking stick of a magician. Dawn on the river. The girl who suckles young lizards stands like a heron between the mangroves. Only the magician's robes are left where he has vanished.

8. (*Mozart's madrigals continue to plague investors. Who will rid me of this bliss?, complain merchants of perishability. A seahorse in sunglasses scoops the floor on Wall Street. Sell now.*)

In the design of her fantastic garden she always left something for dawn to unmake. The tilt of a flower's shadow, a small waterfall half concealed by some felled logs. It is dangerous folly, she said, to compete with the sun's perfection.

9. (*My beautiful native land is there on the margins, a fine-spun fabric of lies in a myopic necromancer's illuminated manuscript.*)

In the new Republic established during Prospero's absence freedom of speech achieves its enduring definition – citizens are free to speak only on topics of which they are completely ignorant. So, on pain of death, lawyers may offer opinions on the growing of cauliflowers but never about laws; farmers on the proper nets to use for deep sea fishing but not about crops or land usage. Whole villages in the great inland desert dispute for hours on the correct way to address a sea urchin. No one who works for the government may talk about the government. No one who teaches may talk about education – they are free to talk about daily life on remote planets provided they have never visited them. Public opinion managers

replace counsellors and statesmen. Meanwhile plague and
war remake the earth.

10. (*Meetings by night on mountain passes. Cinqueterra's journey
to the Eastern Marches interrupted by rival film crews. Fortinbras
and the Afterlife Investment Fund move west.*)

Sent back from Parinirvana he sees:
the golden pulse of the sun spinning
wildly like a potter's wheel, dry
salt-crusted earth and a sagging
banyan hung with voodoo dolls.

11. (*Whoever owns the war owns the fallout. Maverick judge hits
out at neo-Catholic imperialists. A quiet day in Lhasa. Cloud of
knowing promises heavy storms by nightfall.*)

I knew she was a white Russian since
she was wearing a white bikini. In a corner of
the poolside bar the ghost of John Forbes
downs a black Russian, glancing nostalgically
at French sylphs swathed in the flimsiest snippets
of international news. The other side of the veil
of life and death, the fate of the great
Australian poets of the 1970s:
eternal summer sipping on Pink Muscovites:
vodka, grenadine, milk, triple sec,
with a dash of lime and chillies to remind them
of the Tropics.

12. (*A hundred mute gods, their eyes all put out, crowd together on a stone altar. Starved of blood. Lingering on in their hunger for one more sunset. A Sybil dozing lightly in an iron lung prophesies.*)

It may be a day of lunar celebrations in Lhasa but kindly don't treat me as a pretext for gnawing on ravens. Manage your own indigestion with diligence. Not every household fire needs more ghee.

13. (*Elder statesman lounges back on the terrace. Golden fields of insomnia blossom under his gaze.*)

I regret that of myself and all my trembling vulnerability before
the outer limits of beauty
only a riderless horse will reach the basilica where the young
Contessa Laura Mercatore
is singing Mozart's madrigal 129 "The lost staircase"
and that, in the infinite traversal of all worlds,
I will never hear the lips of Bob Hoskins as he intones
the speech of return from all islands
to that quiet inland kingdom known to us only as
"reality." I regret the eyes of the young
Elizabeth Taylor on the forever erased pirate video as she first
    sees
her double the Prince Leonardo DiCaprio
emerge, his doublet soaked from the rough waves
of *The Tempest*.

I regret my late arrival at the Palace of Mirrors
where the fall of a single plate from a table

might have stopped all wars, all death camps.
I regret that I did not purchase my options
in Late Tang Buddhism
or steer the planet on a kindlier course
beyond the Pillars of Mind Control
towards Purgatory's Fortunate Isle where
the Guardians of Forgiveness would have taught us how to see.

14. (*The lights of remote citadels came on all along the windswept seafront. Usurper of the one true sleep asserts, "I have taken charge of the writing."*)

There she was, trailing some scraps of Kant, Germanic and
   beautiful.
Above me, the almond tree spread its immense green sun.

15. (*Small island declares clouds illegal immigrants. Pundits claim: alien water a threat to Fountain of Eternal Ignorance. Border guards urged: no soft landing for stratocumulus freeloaders.*)

Between crumbling buildings
a flag draped on a rock ledge marks a temple.
Flower-studded, the tiers rise
towards the statue of the lone fisherman,
grown old by the river where no fish remain.
A choir of ravens is conducting a funeral.
One by one, they add their wisdom,
these drawn-out notes fading
to form the underlying drone
behind the world.

To enter the stone temple
you must bring a stone.

16. (*The plummet of World Inc. on the Nikkei Index poses question:
what safe haven? At the risk of reigniting urticarial responses,
breathe in deeply the oil-infected mangroves that whisper your
tender secret name heard only in love-making. Spell your hour of
transformation. Magicians' Union threatens walkout. Mass ego-
deflation among balloonists.*)

The squirrels come down to consider us.
Lovingly they examine our offerings.
Alert to all that is,
in an eye's blink they invert their direction
forever improvising a fresh image of transition
like a world suspended
between two languages.

And when the rain fills our hands
and we stand there, lifted
out of ourselves,
what words do we have for that?

17. (*Neither hungover nor handsome. A touch of bad faith
produces unpropitious headache in lower cranial cavity. Eyestrain
for eavesdropper. Nominal investment benefits continue to flow.*)

Like a half-finished tome of suspect theology
used to induce blindness
in unsuspecting acolytes

Like someone waiting on a telephone who hears
the slight plop of a light bulb breaking free from its socket
and the almost simultaneous shattered clarity
of its meeting with the floor
and in an instant they know
the equations they lived within
from now on will bear the imprint
of a punctured eardrum

Like untamed scissors that remove
all greenery from the world

Like the difficult dreams of a time-travelling ant
Like luminous lies

Like the footprints that appear, frost over, then vanish
one winter morning on the ceiling of a monastery
Like a failed runway for grief-laden angels

Like billowing dust clouds that paint the city pink
and leave your mouth sticky

with the spurned soil's reassertion
of pure earth

Like sound investment
Like a mountain that suddenly erupts
all along the dreamer's skin
Like a lifetime's addiction to osmosis

Like a narrow diving board before the great
future stain of your blood against the void

This last request to the Tribunal on Sky-Burials
this incurable nail-biting love
this waiting room before
the Heavenly Emperor's reception chamber

these brittle days

18. (*The rainclouds continue their interminable journey. The
director of internal weather takes a leaf from a bandaged tree and
raises an altar to coconuts.*)

A blur of five languages on the wall of the caravanserai.
The tragedians have arrived – they climb down
from their cart – they know (who
could have told them?) that
a thousand years from now,
directly over their heads,
whales will be slowly swimming north.

19. (*A butterfly flutters in and out of a sarcophagus filled with
honeydew melons. Small birds ride the air like cowboys on
hallucinogens. The Petite Larousse Dictionary of Avian Sign
Language offers no translation.*)

Neglected by all, Hanuman grieves in a frog pond not far
from the deserted temple. Princess Sita has passed beyond the
oceans to a land of ice where no monkeys can live. Hanuman's

friend the Sea Eagle cannot approach that land. Its winds repel all creatures of the great forests. Sita has gone there, an unconscious prisoner hypnotised by a boy in a baseball cap and red and black T-shirt, a boy with all the charm of an unborn planet, gifted with a fine-grained knowledge of those spells that shrink the world.

20. (*Mozart's madrigal "The lost staircase" redefines spiral form in music. Ourselves seen from somewhere out in space. The earth turns. The trees forgive.*)

An island in a lake – in the centre of that island
another lake – nestled in that lake
a further island with a lake,
and so on . . .

On whatever island she may find herself
she takes from her thin plastic bag
a bottle of toxic detangler
to strip from her hair
the ambient sky.

21. (*Oil tankers on the horizon. Ants making hay with the guacamole. Sultan's war canoes approach the enemy's capital under cover of moonless night. A great epic interrupted by urgent household purchases.*)

From far below,
the calling of clear water stirs where a stream
tumbles between underground rocks.

I woke, not as I had foreseen,
in a burning graveyard
but in a small narrow house
across a lane from the city morgue.
Winter sunlight crafted a bent tree.
Sent back from Heaven and Hell,
I was not to be the lover of demons
but to dwell in ordinary time.

22. (*The Russians are making a pyramid in the pool. Meanwhile Sashka sulks, an Arctic Blizzard poised against her lips: white vodka, white rum, white triple sec and a relentless snowstorm of ice.*)

There are small signs along the path
that not all is lost.
Pebbles that resemble
human faces –
into these wide smiles
a steady avalanche of hailstones
is vanishing.

23. (*While Ferdinand sleeps, Miranda gazes into a rough stone mirror of star-crossed water. Dystopic Druids whisper from the depths of the noösphere. Haltingly she scries her face among millennial wreckage. Miranda alone. An arthritic Atlas in ugg boots. Beatific sky-bearer.*)

I come to the edge of my being.
I peer across. I draw the line

that passes through me
into the eddying world.
My father's speech on cosmic accountancy, the true
alignment of Heaven and Hell,
rots in water-laden books
while conmen and their servants,
information managers and gullible gluttons,
find new ways to make the kingdom theirs.
A biplane ferries the murderous twins
to yet another press conference
on fiscal management. Like true villains,
half-benign faces painted on death-riddled skulls,
they have no need
to come onstage.
My mother (the brains of the family)
sleeps in her silver coffin outside D'Este.
I lack the heart to tell my father
all that happens on this island
is the clever chordplay of demented monkeys
while the kingdom we return to,
nestled there beyond the waves,

is some Harvard whizz-kid's
renaming of Nepotism Inc.

In the land I return to
I dream always of the surf-break on the island, the day
my father's magic sprinkled the first dew of wonder
in my fifteen-year-old eyes.

24. (*A small ferry transporting an orchestra of gongs, zithers and transverse nose flutes. The sky glowing pink with the first edges of sunset over the lagoon. He lingered at the helm of his life, as comfortable as a gondolier with a twisted testicle.*)

All day the small round island
had been travelling imperceptibly westward
in pace with the writing.
The sun, as it entered the page before me,
kept changing its language. On the horizon
the island darkened and glowed.
A foretaste. Of infinite oblivion.
When all became as invisible
as the mountain across the strait, I knew my life
must change.

25. (*Abandoned coach found on frozen bridge haloed in mysterious glow. Travelling the ravaged lands Cinqueterra seeks counsel from the astronomer of Prague.*)

Monkeys on the docks at Bremen. Antelope and elk
browse in the suburbs where the cloud has passed.
As in the time of lost migrating mountains
or when the sky burned for five hundred years.
Carbonized heavens. Metallic hail.
We understand a wall of stillness has moved over us.
Our bones are shining in the fields of midnight.

26. (*She was about to cross the street when global market pressures intervened. Starlet in evening gown wings it.*)

Predicting a birth.
Nomad shepherds always in the wrong place.
She lived in a house hidden
from the street's history of winter.
Unbeknownst and in an ill-accoutred hour
she had trifled with the things of magic.
So the last of life is transacted
under a salt-encrusted light-bulb
peppered with flies.

27. (*A shifting creek, a disappearing mountain, the thrice-
invented names melting into the heat-haze. Who are we? Who
have we ever been?*)

At that time the snow was melting and the first storks
in a great arc were wheeling north
against the snow melt. Camping where two rivers meet
the Crusaders of the Vanished God got drunk,
pillaged, raped and murdered for five days.
Deep in the skull of an otter who saw it all
the savage bonfires of a malformed species.

28. (*Wall Street ransacked by delirious cattle. Nocturne of the
disconsolate Vrindaban gopis. The capital left empty, an ideogram
of walls to be read only by the stars.*)

Mild ache in the bones
and a hymn to the benevolent grasslands.
What rises over us
but this tenderness

returning all pain, all folly
to the sky?

29. (*He was destined to be the lover of fifty-five women yet a fatal
flaw held him back.*)

Forever left off-stage, Cinqueterra,
the hero or villain of Shakespeare's great lost tragedy,
recites in endlessly varied voices
the image-clustered lines without ever hearing
the other side of the dialogues. Fashion models, seamstresses,
daughters of oil tycoons and public opinion managers,
all file past the other side of a screen.
His heart pounds but the monologue
is all death-ward.

30. (*Cloud of unknowing hovers over a frog-pond. A pelican with
a stethoscope probes the pulse of the water.*)

Soon we will leave the earth.
Soon the numbness behind my eyes
will send slivers of oblivion
into the smallest wrinkles of the brain.
It is not enough to undertake the ten-month journey
to the tin and canvas shack on the Simpson Desert's
westernmost edge
where Gustav Mahler has lived out his second life,
folding and unfolding
a text of intricately laced Hassidic prayers.
It is not enough to locate the lost music,

or recite an entire 500 Upanishads in Sanskrit
ensuring the breath and mind are focussed
on a single point in space.
Unutterably. The death of all
implicates us.

MARIA ZAFARELLI STREGA
(1961 – ?)

MY ATTEMPTS TO FIND MARIA
ZAFARELLI STREGA

During my partner's absence in Bhutan I went by myself to Buenos Aires in late May 2014 to find out what I could about Maria Zafarelli Strega. I had read the few poems by her included in Alianza Editores' *Antología de Poesía Rioplatense*, originally published in 1993 though I owned the expanded second edition of 2011. I loved the poems, was curious about her and wanted to find out more. It seemed she was still alive, but where? A friend in the film and theatre business in Buenos Aires had suggested an address but no one there had heard of her. Asking at nightclubs and bars in the Palermo district (a suggestion sparked by correspondence with one of the staff at Alianza) eventually brought a result.

After three nights of useless searching, I met a middle-aged woman who gave her name as Carlotta and immediately sparked up at the mention of Maria Zafarelli Strega's name. "Of course I knew Maria," she said. "Buy me another drink and I'll tell you about her." The chill from an open side door drifted across us. Up on stage a rather shrill singer had just finished a round. A noisy group of Spanish tourists had moved on to another nightclub. We settled down at a table in the rear of the bar and she began, "Maria was tough – her life was tough. When she was young she was wealthy, I mean they were all wealthy, her family, but cursed because of that father of hers, a monster if there ever was one. Dead now and anyone might have done it, though I've got my theories. The only really happy time in her life was the summer holidays with her grandparents in Uruguay – at Punta del Este. She'd talk about the huge drop from her grandparents' house to the ocean and the din of cicadas. And then, when she was twelve, her grandparents both died. I don't think she ever got over that shock. She told me too about when she was fourteen and another girl in her class sat on a window ledge to feel the top of her head, found all these bumps and told her she was destined to be a great genius. She never spoke about her father and the terror she and her mother knew because of him – I think she was too frightened ever to talk of that. But, as I said, he's gone now, found in a lane near Teatro Colon with three knives in him. She disappeared just after that." She said this last phrase slowly, with a knowing look I thought, but maybe I'm reading too much into it. "Maria told me she was twenty two," Carlotta went on, "when she finally got free of her father. She'd left secretly for Uruguay, finally ready to become someone else – the only way she could ever be herself. It was tough, her three years in Montevideo. Moving from place to place, half-starved sometimes, looking for cheap places to eat or sleep or escape from it all with alcohol or pills, mostly in Aguada and Villa Muñoz, never that far from the Estación General Artigas – that was when she met Aurélie, the great love of her life. But if you know about Maria you know about Aurélie. I don't want to talk about Aurélie – if you know how it ended it's too painful to talk about, and maybe I'm jealous – maybe I hoped somewhere I would be loved like that. But I was never Maria's type. We got to know each other around the time she and Aurélie broke up, after she'd tried to kill herself with barbiturates. But I don't want to talk about that." And at that Carlotta looked worried, confused, downed her drink, swept everything into her handbag, and prepared to leave. "I forgot. I should be somewhere else. Come back tomorrow night and I'll meet you here. I don't want to talk any more but you can see the scraps of writing she left me. It's all I have of hers . . . she never liked photos." And with that she rose to her feet and, slightly the worse for her several drinks, vanished into the chill late autumn night.

The next day I went back to the bar and waited and waited. At one in the morning there was still no sign of her so I left. I returned the next night and waited. When she hadn't turned up by twelve thirty I started to leave. We almost collided in the door as Carlotta walked in, making no apologies as if the missed night had not existed. Once we were seated at the same table in the rear of the bar she produced from her handbag a battered dog-eared copy of a French edition of *Aurélia* by Gérard de Nerval. And, as I opened the front cover, there on the title page was the word "Aurélia" surrounded by hand-drawn stars and a strange shape that on closer inspection was a bolt of lightning severing a pigeon into two parts. Flipping through the book I saw pasted onto various pages small cards covered in what I took to be Maria's handwriting, at times in a peculiarly disjointed Spanish. Were these really the writings of Maria Zafarelli Strega, the poet born in September 1961 whose whereabouts had been unknown since 1995? Her name was written on the front cover, in a neat miniature script that certainly looked like the one letter of hers I had been shown from the archives at Alianza Editores or, to my mind, like the scrawl on a handful of similar cards later brought out by the owner of a bookshop on Calle Florida, another enthusiast of her poetry whom I met through introductions from my film and theatre friend, Fernando. (When I spoke to the woman at the bookshop a few days later, shortly before flying back to Australia, she gave the impression she was tired of the mysterious disappearance and the endless speculations. She seemed fairly certain that if Maria had disappeared it was because Maria had wanted to disappear. After all, she said, the years of the dictatorship were long gone and there seemed little reason to suspect foul play, and yet?)

Carlotta spoke very little that second night, content to give me time to read the notes, and, with her permission, I copied down several of the cards. There were many I barely glanced at, cards with only phone numbers, names of people, individual disjointed words or phrases scrawled in ways I could not decipher. They seemed to point towards a privacy I already felt should be left as privacy. It was Maria's writings as a poet I was interested in. I already felt I had come as close as I ever would to the real Maria. Her thin volume of poems I have never been able to track down – only 100 copies were produced in 1988 and there have been no re-issues. It is only her poems in the Anthology I have ever been able to find. The fragments I found on the cards I will reproduce (in translation) here. I was struck by the strangeness with which she wrote about herself, almost always, in the third person, not unlike the poem in the Alianza Anthology titled "From the notebooks of Maria Zafarelli Strega."[2]

---

2 Only later on the plane back to Sydney did I recall a certain phrase used by Ana, the woman in the bookshop, "Sometimes when people disappear they stay exactly where they are." It occurred to me that, if Maria had changed her name once, she could do so again and for a few moments I wondered, but it seemed too crazy a thought, could Carlotta be Maria?

THE CARD COLLECTION

MZF's vertiginous reinvention of herself began at age 22 on a sidewalk near the Cementerio del Norte in Montevideo, a cold morning in mid-winter. She no longer had a name – that baggage of evil had fallen into the sea on the ferry from Buenos Aires – and for three days she had wandered the city without a name. That morning she saw it appear all by itself on a shop window frosted over by 6 am chill: Maria Zafarelli Strega. Her name.

She heard only the sounds no one hears.

Poor Maria. If she could just climb out of herself and step down into the other world. Then she could love.

She always dreamed of living in Paris but every time she saved up money to go there someone would break into her flat or strangers would steal it. Even when she had no flat, even when she had no money. She was destined to survive here only or not at all.

It will not be easy to be born under the earth. I have heard plants tell me that.

An ordinary evening in the park near Paseo de Florida. She was invited by two mice to accompany them and she tracked her way across the park into a deserted building, the two mice constantly looking back to make sure she was following. Once she entered the building, they wanted her to go down into their underground burrow and she had to explain patiently that this was not possible. And from the window, just above her, the leaden weight of the sky kept trying to force her to surrender.

For a whole month during the bitterest winter of my memories, in a hovel near the docks I would unfold my map of Paris. The two working girls who let me stay there marveled at the joy I took in my map. I would say out loud, I will write this novel on this street, on this street I will write a poem, at a bar near this corner I will begin my most famous book. And I would imagine making my way through the curves and steep tunnels of lanes leading to Père Lachaise or heading across the Marais. The two girls watched with incredulity as I played with the map. I was at some time the lover of both girls but we did not make love anymore. Our bodies had become too strange, too much a tangled skein of catastrophes. I remember once kissing the long scar that trailed down one girl's belly.

I remember a very drunken dawn when one of them tried to kiss the knot of pain that kept exploding deep under my skull. When they made it back to the room at dawn after all the clients of the afternoon and the night, after working the streets and sometimes being kicked and beaten, they came back to sleep.

Years later I had a much older woman who was my lover. When she left me she said, "I have made this for you. Lay this small sack of herbs over your eyes and you'll find sleep. Someday you'll see. When you can't give love anymore, at least you can give sleep."

I was destined to survive here only, to invent my name, to discover almost nothing – but that slender thread would be everything.

Self-sabotaging faces in a frosted mirror at dawn.
We were breathless like the wire of the sky.

When the cat came to play with me and I had to explain that I would be dying soon it understood everything straightaway. Everything I could never explain to people was clear straight away. And because words were almost unnecessary, new playful words migrated into my head or suddenly were just there, secreted by some twist in a vein or fold of tissue, puffed up there and then like balloons in the vexing inner chamber of my head. The words were not audible. I simply saw them, like the words of my new name that just wrote themselves out before me one morning. They made me remember things that came from another world.

She was being driven out along the magical bridge of the seven rivers. River after river flowed slowly by under the narrow bench of her carriage while, in front, the driver sat idly flicking a knot of string into the air above the horse that shifted a little forward every few moments. An immense dawn sky stretched in layers of gold and pink interrupted by wisps of cloud, but there were no birds. She wondered why in all the teeming flow of waters there were no birds, and why the silence of the world was so total. "India" she thought to herself, and here she was, being driven towards this secret India devoid of people, this plain of silent rivers and limitless dawn.

Each river she crossed was less than a river – it was as if every river had been shredded into thin ribbons of water in an inexhaustible plain. Is this the Ganges or the pampas, she wondered. "Nous voyageons vers l'Orient mais nous sommes en 'Oriente'," she said to herself in French, using the old Argentine name for Uruguay, and then, counting each separate stream she was passing, she thought, "When the sequence of finite numbers has run out I will wake up at my grandmother's house in Punta del Este."

Waiting out the grey wind. Sometimes I wake and I think: it is somewhere. In a small box slipped under the floorboards of the stairs, my blue wish, my breath. What came out of my eyes one night, what hid away.

At a certain time I had to say, No, I will not go any further down the dark road. I will stop just here, under this tree, and write for two days, then I will die. And the two days grew and grew and started to look, almost, like a lifetime.

Along the flat endless road where I walk, sheltered from the brisk wind by fragrant burning piles of cow-dung, I stop beside a small one-room house where I catch sight of a tiny mirror dangling from the ceiling. Stepping through the doorway, I am suddenly in a corridor of whirling mirrors, each turning at different angles at different speeds as if in answer to a multitude of undetectable breezes, a myriad of off-centered climates or micro-whirlwinds that arise only in private deserts. Fearfully I step among them and my face slips into one mirror while my hands, my legs are elsewhere. I am enjoying my fractured loneliness when a woman steps from behind a curtain. She is wearing purple gauze and a conical blue hat that is topped with the sign of the moon. "It is all frightfully simple," she says. "You just choose." And her smile slides back and forth between a wide gentleness and a knowing carnivorous intensity. Between the small circling diamonds of glass I freeze and I wonder, Am I she?

Who is it who comes to me, who is almost known, almost visible, almost might leave a glance inside me, a thumb print on a wall, a name, even just a single word, now in extremis as a curtain falls back into place when the breeze stops, something or someone whose gliding past brushes me, glare of the one day so awful, yet needing to be stayed with, this absolute face I yearn for, the longest arc of days, washing of the sea through the window, wave on grey wave tilting towards the end of vision, almost slightly, who?

Yesterday all day rats circling round me – first in the rat eyes of the old woman nibbling at the fingers and toes of the children caught in the sugar house, then in the two small sandals worn by the woman eaten by rats. When all that is left is terror and hunger. When we are both the rat with its numbed eyes and the victim unable to escape, a starved body nailed to a bed of collapse. In the distance the rising falling notes of the legendary piper who would lead away our nightmare. A music in the world's far corner that holds the key to our unsuspected otherness. The part of us already elsewhere.

POEMS FROM THE ALIANZA ANTHOLOGY *POESÍA RIOPLATENSE CONTEMPORANEA*

FROM *THE NOTEBOOKS OF MARIA ZAFARELLI STREGA*

1.

Despite the monsters we are here.
Such small threads have lassoed a distant star
to a mirror of ice.
Who are we to be graced
with this clumsy incomprehensible abundance?

We barely walk the road of the sky.
Hobbled by the world,
this ecstasy.

2.

I don't know how I manage to live
so crowded out by them —
no one released to heaven
since those doors shut firm millennia ago.
Always there are more of them,
and they keep invading each thing I touch,

each plank I move across
hemmed in to right and left
as I go on, letting more and more escape me,
simplifying down till I have to vacate
every memory
and live only in the question
"Who am I?"
but even that bewilderment
comes to me battered by this throng of faces and voices,
this distorting shifting mirror
that repeats:

even as pure absence
you have nowhere to go.

3.

For now
they have hauled us out of a difficult heaven.
Fish-hooked by the stars.
Bent-double people.
Sifted through the sky people.
In this thin air.

4.

In the Book of Lions the cavern opened out.
And the soul descended a long staircase,

hearing always further ahead
the soft waters of oblivion.
Each fall lifts the heart.
Each notch of darkness
promises the sky.

You are the woman I see in my tiny hand-mirror.
Your lips bear the beauty of the dead.

ASPHYXIA

On the hill the black sky chokes the purple house
my cry goes out
to no one

I will drink the glass of water
My death is teeming there –
a red vibration, the signature
of fractured eyes

Tuesday climbs the hill
slopping pails of skulls

SPELLS

On all the receivers when I leave my number
I feel I am leaving some secret
sliver of myself –
an imprint from the labyrinth within me
and now I will never find my way
through it.

Everything else sheds in order to grow back
but I diminish and diminish
as I make my way to the smallest
remotest island
at the end of all islands.

Knot this dream onto your nightmare.
Let your handkerchief hold the three teeth
stolen from the drowned girl's face.

AT THE GRANDPARENTS

Two doors down
you reigned your cheerful notes
in tune with the faint ringing of a sherry glass
as your smile leant over
the pink tilted head of the parrot
meditative and omniscient in his perched cage.
How he rocked, his white salt tongue
tainted by the sea that lurched
always at your shoulder in the window
while we munched your sweets,
slightly frightened like Hansel and Gretel
in your stucco biscuit house.
The dizzy green drop beyond your garden
was all the length of summer falling
to the sea
and when we left at the front gate
our eyes fell step by step into the stillness
where jasmine, frangipani and that
green creeping abundance that has no name
jostled our senses.
The red paint on my grandparents' front fence
stays unflaking in memory
long after all our deaths.
And my eyes still crave the sea.

IN THE END

the paper shines through
so that now
from the vastness of the book in front of me,

from all its
never-to-be-unscrambled subplots,
this empty silent being-here

is its gift.

THE SANDPITS OF EDEN

Will the elongated whale with the long tooth stuck in its
    forehead
ever stop prowling the midnight corridors of my brain?

Do you hear me, Jonah?
Are you carrying Nineveh within you
as a present for the King of Kings?

Will the whale find my secret room?
When it does will I too be Jonah?

Am I Jonah already?
Is this why my neck feels wrung out,
the smell of krill leaking from my hair?

Is my house a whale fixed to the earth by stone cables,
groaning as it tries to swim free?

Are my fingers evidence?
Does their unmistakeable chill come from trying to filter the
    universe,
to sift out dust specks that are remnants
of soaring angels and exploding nebulae?

Must I always be starting over, naked and bruised
from my passage through a thousand bodies,
all excrement and the fragrance of jasmine buds?

Am I the great polar lake in its ring of ice or the whale that
   dreams it?

Who will answer for me when I am vomited out
in the sandpits of Eden?

AN INTRODUCTION TO A NEW GAME

In the lower right-hand corner of this map
is the Kingdom of Sleep.
Unlike some other board games you may know
we do not consider ourselves a preparation
for this final state.
The small brown faces with trusting eyes
you can make out if you peer carefully
into the wandering bowls of ice
are sea-deer, the bringers of good fortune.
There is no way to attract them, no way
to predict when they might give
their calm infusions of benevolence.
Look at the Admiral – he offers firm advice –
do not go near him
for the price of his order-talismans
is instant burial.
Sometimes the roar of the dead will be
all you hear:
at such times leave the board,
burn incense in each room of your house,
leave food-offerings on all windowsills
and silver coins by the front and rear doors.
Return only when you hear the first notes
of the bird that promises imminent daybreak.
Can you see four slowly-breathing fingers
that carry a pen trapped in their mouth:
should you add this to your toolbox

it may bring happiness or madness
but hardly a durable salvation.
Even now the cold night breeze
rattles the flimsy map.
The game invites.
It comes with no special recommendation.

THE THREE WOMEN

They stand outside the house in green shadow:
three women from another age:
one is tall with a doubtful face, one I cannot see,
one holds a basket of plums.

The sky is made of stone: smooth and streaked in cloud:
it feels like ancient blocks that hold us in.

Tomorrow, if the sun crosses my threshold,
I will be a child again: held tight in a wave's echo.

In the green world of now
a white rose drops from its stem,
a bell on a church tower sounds –

three women fall silent, look away,
someone's shadow has just passed.

WHAT IS

The face so beautifully intense
mirrors a world outside life.
Horrors have rained down like hammers
and distant stars like griefs
shine in the lines of fingers.

They trawl us.
We are sucked into
a slow breathing nowhere.

From a tiny cloud over the right temple
they watch us, the kindly elders.
Above the white worn-out lip
a single tooth protrudes

while the head, so small now, is all
marching orders
for the long slog into
forgetting.

FEDERICO SILVA
(1901 – 1980)

Federico Silva (born in Tours in 1901 and died in Madrid 1980) was a little known painter, writer of abandoned novels and a small collection of poems. In Paris during the 1920s, he was a sometime acquaintance of Erik Satie, Michel Leiris and the young René Char. While living in Madrid he translated extensively from Spanish to French, being especially interested in the poets emerging in the 1950s and later. The Cuban concert violinist, Antonieta Villanueva, a good friend of musicians like Ricardo Viñes, Alicia de Larrocha and Federico Mompou, was his companion in his later years. His Catalan background may be spurious, nevertheless he chose to write poetry in that language under the pseudonym Umberto Suarez.

EXCERPTS FROM THE UNFINISHED MEMOIRS *DU CÔTÉ DE VERCINGETORIX* (TRANSLATED FROM THE FRENCH)

by Federico Silva (also known as Umberto Suarez)

Nothing was quite like the garden at Vercingetorix. Some days it stretched for an acre and a half running into the wilderness of a thickly timbered state forest leased, more or less permanently, to the military who, without building anything beyond a few overgrown woodland tracks, would from time to time issue pronouncements asserting its strategic importance to the homeland's defence against Italian submarines, Moorish gunboats or Carthaginian pirates. On other days we would wake to find the garden shrunk to no more than a row of pot plants on a balcony while the still uncompleted frames of a projected housing estate jostled against a makeshift bamboo fence, a crazy piece of exotica brought back by my father's half-brother from one of his many excursions to our colonies in the East. On the days when it occupied an acre and a half of land we would wander through its dense uncanny rain forest, following the uneven marble slabs of a meandering circular path, pausing to breathe in the sunlight on the two arched bridges that took us over a swift shallow creek. I remember the first time we walked astounded through this landscape, pausing dumbstruck to gaze up at the two waterfalls – one at the top of the garden near the house, one far down in the gully perched above a disused tennis court that had disappeared into a field of abandoned flowering vegetables. Elsewhere lantana, monsterio, bracken and assorted vines kept taking over the garden and, whenever they were hacked back, they would reveal some new pathway or marble feature. The creek carved a long diagonal across the property and, on the ridge line farthest from the house, there was a cluster of sandstone boulders shielding a narrow barely discernible cave and, just beyond it, concealed by a stand of tall trees and the ubiquitous tangle of lantana, there appeared, as if shimmering under a different sun, a neat rectangle of carefully tended lawn, a neighbour's house with a ship's masthead planted in the centre of the lawn from which at all times the Norwegian flag fluttered so that we had only to crawl our way through the lantana, then step over a low line of shrubs to enter Norway. Also, in one corner of the garden, there was a glasshouse filled with my mother's orchids. These were the magical flowers that would later accompany us children wherever we moved, travelling with my sisters to the different houses they lived in after their marriages, one sister in the northwest of Paris, one in a run-down villa near Urbino, one in an apartment in Madrid, and for my four brothers spreading out across France and Europe the orchids went with them in a diaspora of pale white and pink openness. For my own part, my mother's orchids (at least five of them) have journeyed through the many houses I have lived in, flowering in seven cities and as many lifetimes.

Tended occasionally by himself but mostly by the various gardeners he would hire in his intermittent bursts of horticultural enthusiasm, my father's garden had the marvellous property of changing its size. My father could never explain this but urged us never to speak of it to others.

Until now I have never used the private name he gave to our house "Vercingetorix" – as if to highlight some undefeated realm, something that would never fall to the Rome of reason. It is only now, many years after his death and approaching my own death, that I feel it is safe to write of these things. I have wondered how it was that the wind would bring us days when the whole ornamental garden, the abandoned fantasy of a magnate in the printing and publishing trade, the inventor of a new kind of greeting card, of elaborate board games and the projected universal encyclopaedia of childhood, would shrink to a strip of narrow lawn and a flowerbed or simply the balcony itself. Monsieur Sable, the printing magnate, had apparently designed everything himself according to some scheme he alone understood but died when his mansion had been scarcely begun, leaving his widow at the centre, or rather the extreme left edge, of an unmanageable chaos. No one local, no one who knew the story or the rumours, would buy the house, but my father, an outsider desperate for a place large enough for his brood of eight children, was immensely pleased to "snap up the place for a song" as he put it one day to his incredulous father-in-law. Certainly there were days when everything about the house shrank, as if here we children had to learn to contend with slipping into the future. Certainly the space and freedom of those early years of the century would vanish steadily so that by the fifties and sixties none of us could offer our own children a fraction of what we had known in the apparently eternal time of childhood.

The garden was my father's realm, the sea my mother's. I grew up between them. From our house it was possible to reach two beaches by taking very different walks. The closest beach could be reached in ten minutes; the further beach, a leisurely forty minutes walk, offered more spectacular opportunities for play and held greater mystery for us as we turned fourteen and fifteen with its forbidden sealed-off girls' boarding school in a nearby back-street from which at times squads of young girls in grey and red uniforms would emerge. At one end of this beach there was a boat ramp, jutting out across rocks with passages of deeper water spliced between them, and into this labyrinthine darkness we would navigate the one canoe we shared among us, taking it in turns to lie flat and unmoving as the canoe, sped erratically by currents and waves, bumped its way through the narrowest of openings. There, below the wooden frame of the boat ramp, we entered the darkness, a counter-world to the glaring midday sun. The water itself changed its nature in that darkness; its sounds were louder, it bristled with crabs and starfish, it teemed with the stringed feelers of jellyfish or tiny darting fish that had no names. Lying there completely still, catching distorted glimpses of the sky visible in streaks above the lattice of the jetty, I discovered how, by moving into darkness, the time of everything could be slowed down. Under the creaking of a boatshed ramp, the pontoon that rose and fell with the slap of waves, in a darkness made far darker by the glare of the sun outside, everything stretched out, gaining the quality of being a non-repeatable world. I remember one day coming out from that darkness and gazing directly at the sun. As I turned away, I saw two black circles and below them brief paragraphs of words, the small words linking larger words. Below one circle I imagined I saw the phrase "death and other synonyms for truth." Below the other circle quite distinctly I recognised, with the flourishes of its capital L, "Life" which stood in a small forest of words none of which I can remember. Closing my eyes again, I lay completely still in the darkness of no words at all. Resting there a while I remembered the phrase "the needy one," that had been one of the names in the vanishing paragraph, and a story about someone who fell through a hole in the world and found himself talking to the stars in the very cold air near the cliffs when morning came.

One day, returning from the closer beach, we took a deliberate wrong turning and ended up on the path above the Bay of Stars. As we came round a sudden corner in the meandering road we were at once face to face with a monastic-looking building of many tall windows, an out-of-place red-brick mansion perched on a cliff. It was the shuttered structure of the House of Dreamers, a late 19th century secret society of sorts, that built this mansion overlooking the sea, then a few years later disappeared. They believed that, through long immersion in dreaming, the adepts of their group could commune with the archetypal world-shapers and so predict the coming of the New Jerusalem. According to some prophecies, because this place above the Bay of Stars was at the exact opposite corner of the Mediterranean to Jerusalem, the second coming of Christ would happen here, some said in the year 1900, others in 1911 or 1922.

Many years later I was living in exile in Madrid. I was at that time supporting myself by teaching French while trying to sell an assortment of aquarelles and gouaches I had painted. I had read an announcement of a small exhibition of paintings by Matisse to be held in a tiny gallery in the far north of the city in a region I had never visited. That night was so rainy and stormy I had thought to forget about my outing and go back to the *pension* where I lived, but the prospect of seeing paintings of the south, of sun and the Mediterranean, was too powerful an attraction in that long cold Madrid winter. I sat in a bus that was making its slow way up Calle de Velazquez under lights refracted in rain. The trees, draped in fairy lights at the approach of Christmas, leaned close across the road. Paying the modest fee I entered the gallery – in a far corner I saw it, a painting by Matisse of what I instantly recognised as the garden at Vercingetorix.

~Ø~

So far from the Mediterranean. I am nine or ten – my father waking me in a cabin on the ferryboat from Bergen to Kristiansund (he had taken me along as a treat on one of his business trips.) "Look," he said, "you may never see this again – the northern lights." We gazed then into the north as if we stood together at the edge of the universe. Far beyond and overhead and all around we saw them – end-shimmerings.

~Ø~

My childhood, as it lives within me, happened entirely in the sun, but it did not start out that way. Before we came to Vercingetorix we lived in the cold inland city of Tours which in my memory, aside from one vivid summer, was a place of perpetual rain. A few years after we came to Vercingetorix, at the lycée we eventually began attending, I was asked to give a speech before the class. I was told to speak of something very clear to me, something I could touch and feel – and at once I saw myself standing outside a bread shop in Tours, my last winter there, a grey evening, for evenings came so quickly there, and I was sheltered under an awning as torrents of rain fell on the street. Clutching the warm bread tightly to me, I waited a short while for the worst of the rain to pass. I could have picked at the bread a little as I was hungry but the scent of its still burning centre and the warmth were so strong I felt no need to eat. Held by that fragrance and that warmth even more tightly than my hands held the bread, I sensed that, while the substance of the bread, the white air-spun texture of survival, would pass through me, the fragrance and the warmth were now lodged deep inside me. In Tours with its grey streets and dark shuttered houses I had to learn to guard whatever there was of the sun's fire in some inner place closer than memory, and I had also learnt how strong that inner fire could be. I don't remember giving the speech that day in the lycée, the erased surface of the chalkboard looming behind me, for I was outside myself all the time I was speaking, completely surrounded by the sound of rain. I only remember a burst of applause from other students and the surprised look on my teacher's face as I sat down.

~Ø~

More memories of Tours. A primary school outing: a fancy dress party by a lake, for the headmistress of the school was an enthusiast for the imaginary participation in the lives of animals. Trapped inside the suit of a cat, the mask pulled down so my altered eyes alone look out. As my breathing tightens, the horror that I would never come back from some place entirely outside the human. Likewise the fear produced by a play where I saw how the English words "now" and "here" fused into "nowhere," so that to touch anything exactly in space and time simultaneously would cause one to be transposed across some line into vanishing. For Tours was not only the city of rain but the city of nightmares.

~Ø~

My father was a businessman. Many months of each year he was away on business trips – Paris, Brussels, London, sometimes Cologne, Hamburg or Zurich. I understood little of his business deals – he insisted to my mother that everything was legitimate and above board but it was true that he had alternate names, a plethora of business cards and several quite different outfits he would wear. "I carry out my promises," he said, "and I know how to put the right people together but often it is first necessary to make an impression – the right clothes, the right sounding name, they let you get your foot in the door. As long as you do what you say you will, business people don't really care what your name is, though social habit requires the pretence of a fixed identity. It is also true," he added, "that my own father had several names, so how can I tell who I am?" He would then say, turning mysteriously towards us children, "One day I will tell you about your grandfather."

Occasionally, as I reached my teens, he would take me for a week or so on one of his trips to see the world, as he said. In Vercingetorix we all felt equal – not just my brothers and sisters but those outside the family too. We had no servants though Madame Morrice would help my mother a few days a week with the cleaning and other jobs. I remember the shock when I first discovered social class and the horrible differences it made whether you were rich or poor. It was in Paris that I first saw beggars in the streets.

~Ø~

How did I know – did I know? – that the place I went to visit that night (not yet twenty-two, bundled into the back of a friend's car, the roads covered in mist, the chill of invisible roads, stepping across a patch of frozen lawn, an opening door, the small dishevelled room in a tumbledown house, my friend's ex-lover greeting him cautiously beyond the threshold) the drizzle of midnight rain, a tree leaning out into mist, everything leaning above an abyss behind us: the house, my cowered friend swathed in his cap against the cold, his ex-lover's brief glance, the whiteness of her skin as she readjusted the wrappings round the baby she was nursing: that all this which, had there been light, would have shimmered in a blue ice-bound lake, was less than a ten minute walk from the small private hospital where, thirty years later, (was this already held, mirrored in advance by the sheen of lake water?) gazing into thin trees from a bed moved up beside the window, struggling for the air he could no longer swallow, his puzzled distorted face trying to articulate my mother's name, that last night after he had fallen asleep and we went out to watch the stars, sometime before dawn my father stopped breathing.

INTRODUCTION TO A SELECTION OF POEMS BY FEDERICO SILVA

As mentioned previously, Federico Silva wrote poetry in Catalan under the name Umberto Suarez. Initially I had decided not to include the poetry as the work from the late 1920s and 30s under the name of Suarez seemed to me rather disappointing compared to Silva's prose. Late in 2014, however, I came across a thin French edition of his poems. At first I assumed they were merely translations of the Catalan poems I'd already read. Instead these were late poems, written in French during the 1960s and 70s. Quite different in style and tone from his early work, they reflect his own life in a far more obvious way, as I recognised from having read parts of his journals.

A recurrent theme in the journals is his grief at the death of his mother. She died in her home outside Tours in 1942 while Federico was cut off, taking refuge from the Vichy authorities in Spain. By the end of the war the family home with parents and eight children, the whole magic world conjured in "The Garden at Vercingetorix," was gone forever. The poem "The well" evokes that loss. A second source of grief was the end of his marriage when in 1938 his Canadian wife took the two children, then aged nine and ten, and returned to Toronto. With the war and his wife's remarriage it was not until 1952 that he met his daughter again. "Houses for rent (two moments in a marriage)" deals in part with that whole period of his life. I was taken aback by the mention in the poem of grevillea and fruit bats, which I thought only existed in Australia, but grevillea is also endemic to New Caledonia from where an uncle had brought back cuttings, just as he had brought a menagerie of fruit bats from Greece where they also live. The style of this poem is, I believe, decidedly Catalan or Spanish, owing something to the plain-speaking tradition associated with Jaime Gil de Biedma or Gabriel Ferrater or, equally, with Italian poet Cesare Pavese. A more playful approach is evident in "The translator's eyesight" or the quasi-surrealist "Climbing the staircase of water." It is curious that, settling in Madrid, where he lived with the then-severely-disabled Antonieta Villanueva[3], he began writing poems in French but marked by Spanish influences whereas, previously, living in France and under the spell (perhaps too strong a spell) of French poets, he wrote in Catalan. Whether it was the change in languages, the adoption of a more congenial style or simply greater maturity, these final poems strike me as far more interesting than the various collages, concrete poems and collections of puns that fill his first two volumes.[4]

---

3 The reader will meet Antonieta Villanueva later in this book where excerpts from her Memoirs are presented.

4 I had thought I was being rather unfair to Silva's Catalan poetry but very recently came upon the following remarks in Villanueva's *Memoirs*, Volume II. I would be the first to admit her comments are rather one-sided and exaggerated, but still I find them interesting: "I never liked those books from the 1930s, *Jocs d'una sargantana de l'estiu* and *Grillons d'una taronja de foc*,* and I was never afraid to tell Federico so. I couldn't see him in them at all. Too much Michel Leiris. It's true that in his Preface he was the first one to use the word 'constraints' and I claim he invented the term 'usine poétique', not Roussel. But how dull all that experimentalism was. They were so in love with inventing procedures for mass-producing poetry they forgot there has to be actual life in there. In music the inventors of new forms didn't just stop and say 'Look at me, I'm the first person to use a xylophone combined with a washbasin', as if that was all there was to music. Think of Bartok's last piano concerto or Poulenc's late chamber music. Or Messaien's Quartet. For them innovation was simply a fresh way to channel the stuff that really matters – the horror, the beauty, the delicacy, the silence. When I saw 'The well' I knew Federico had found a voice. He'd finally got over competing for 'novelty.' He'd become a poet."

*Games of a summer lizard and Slices of a fiery orange.

POEMS BY FEDERICO SILVA

THE WELL

Far below in the valley
a small light glitters –
the pilot light of the underworld
shining from the earth-bound well
where my mother lives.

I am at the airport waiting for my cousin to arrive
bringing the sealed urn with the elixir
direct from Florida.
We will sprinkle it over her face:
ageing will stop, she will grow young again
and we will pour what remains in the urn
over the ashes of our house
and it will come back:
my brothers and I will be sitting there
at the long table,
around us space will hang
suspended for one moment
as paint grows back, laughter ricochets above us,
buried tins of long-lost regrets
reappear in cupboards –

and a single peal of my mother's voice
will be there

sounding in the ear of each of us –
her voice
like flakes of bread made golden in a light
unknown to any of us
will settle into the deep furrows
over the eyebrows of each of our children
while our own voices chase

the whirlwind of dust.

OF MEMORY

In the bedroom one of the cupboard doors swung open and
the tattered coat of the late Princess shimmered with its halo
of moths. There was no moon but a streetlight crossed the
floor. Have you forgotten me already? It was my great-aunt's
voice meek as a bowl of milk left out for the cats that lived
in the vacant lot behind her house when my father let his car
wander through all the least reputable streets of the port. If
you hold out for me I will insert this folded message in your
prayer book (I promised her spirit) and I will put the key to
the whiskey cabinet back in the pocket of your dress. I never
saw her but I felt her soft blue eyes fuse into my jet-black eyes
and, in the dining room at the far end of the corridor, shards
of ice landed all by themselves on the sideboard beside the
half-empty flask of whiskey. I said her name. Irène.

CLIMBING THE STAIRCASE OF WATER

The fish generate the immense music of night.
To their prayers I owe my being.
The ladders and stairwells of the riverbank
rise spontaneously from the incantations they make
sifting through silt and the drifting
water-plants of darkness.

Let no one willfully deny
the elongated reach of their night vision.
Let no one slight their omniscience.
Ignorant of their silent appraisals of stars and seasons
sleek striding monsters press onward
in the busy task of self-destruction.

Fish, tiny divine
creatures of air and compacted fire,
you live also in my blood.
Processors of the universe,
the way ahead trails in bubbles from your mouth.
This night for the first time
I have seen you.
Silent composers, humming masters
of wordless oratorios,
you know but will never say
the twists and turns, all the
small kinks of my veins,
what flows far within me

and, from the world's first day, bears
the gleaming light of my death.

THE TRANSLATOR'S EYESIGHT

calzar: to put on one's shoes; *cazar:* to hunt
– Spanish Dictionary

I misread "cazando" as "calzando" so error
leads the poem in new directions.
How else would the mice learn to put on their shoes,
button their after-dinner jackets, fold
the graven tablets of protocol and assess
the pink line of twilight reddening
above the sea, weighed now
with a sombre and eloquent dispassion?

In one glance the mice take in
a candle-flame trembling on a window-ledge
and, beyond, a curve of ocean,
a small naval vessel turning
its grey shoulder to the last
flickers of a summer sky.

And like the naval vessel I turn,
buffeted by misdirection, to catch
my reflection in an off-balance gaze,
myopic. My dress shoes
hunting words that still escape me.
My borrowed mice eyes
seeing the world made new.

HOUSES FOR RENT

(two moments in a marriage)

1.
We climb the stairwell to the upper room
that has no door, that is all
undivided bedroom, bathroom, study
with windows open on all sides –
the sense of every vein being left
on display.
The empty house bristles with garish paint.
I look out into scrub and a sad
fake Roman temple.
There is a story of fire
and I can tell it's more than fire
that's ravaged here.
I remember the sounds of breakage and rage,
the dock at Le Havre,
on the last night the eyes of the children.
In the gully below
among the life-worn boulders
hawks and a lone grey eagle
swirl and chatter.
I will cross the sea again
and build her a home beyond the wildest breakers.
How do I know
how far into the darkness
I would be willing to drive?

2.
(On holidays)

Mid-afternoon in midsummer.
In the rented apartment
the children have changed and are
jumping and wriggling in their swimmers
to go down the steep stairwell
and enter the rockpool.
In the surfside garden the palm trees
are already the jilted emblems of
happiness.

Now fruit bats
are squabbling and gliding
among the grevillea, holding their noisy
nocturnal assizes. You read out
the stars that circle us,
the names of constellations
and the friendly visitors of light.

JEUNES FILLES AU JARDIN

for Antonieta

Summer. Cloudless sky.
I guide your wheelchair down the steep busy hill,
past the fountain at Cibeles to the Retiro's
reed-lined lake.
It is August 1961 and I am sixty
and, from behind us, the cries of young girls
come towards us. The shrillness
of their voices brushes our hair
like lost hands that still caress
the sunlight's rich texture.
        Soon under the acacia's leaves
you are reading me a fresh installment of your memoirs.
And I see your twelve-year-old self
hesitant, encased in one of those
frilled many-layered dresses
girls wore in those times. Havana afternoons.
Warm twilight on the edge of formal gardens.
Discretely you lift to your lips
the crushed coolness of guava and mango
while, outside, the fountain's wayward spray
lightly dusts your classmates as they chatter.
        Above Madrid's restless traffic
last night, hearing Alicia play, suddenly
I heard their soft whispering once more
and saw you in your twelve-year-old dress.
Their voices, your face

trapped forever in five rising falling notes.
It is Federico Mompou. *Girls in the garden.*

THE LONG DRIVE TO THE END OF THE SKY

In the sixteenth year of his death
my father drives out along the wind-blown peninsula
beyond the whirling canebreaks, the glittering
ancient sandbanks where signposts and roads
lose their knowledge of human spaces
and birds and rodents watch us with heat-laden eyes.
We kids are in the back and all our later lives,
our mistakes, have been wiped clean,
lightly falling away like dead skin
from sun-burnt noses.

Care-worn as always,
my mother waits for our return
in the deep well where she now lives.
However anxious she is on the inside, for us
her face will register only the statement
that all is well. My father is flicking
between stations on the radio as he
always did, simultaneously following
a dozen news reports in four languages
and criticizing each one.

A cloud follows us, half white half
darkness and charged with
that dry summer lightning that is
the flavour of our eternal identity.
And there is somehow a waterfall

we drive through and drive beyond
into a cool sub-alpine climate
where a rainbow has brushed
the forever unchanging leaves
of pines, eucalypts and cedars.
Abundance is our life here
at the end of the sky.

LAZLO THALASSA
(ADDITIONAL TRANSLATIONS)

SELECTED POEMS FROM *EL SEÑOR L'AMOROSO AND OTHER STRANGERS*

THE ENTRANCE OF L'AMOROSO AT THE GRAND CONCOURSE FOR SKELETONS.

1.

The plane came in limping down the runway.
Arriving for the banquet of the skeletons,
L'Amoroso (his woven bag filled
with parchments, sonnets and sonatas, the plumed
articulation of a wild bird's soaring) crosses
the tarmac, glides through
the trembling doors: fragrant bursts
of pine forest, of dark earth
and rising ocean mist, ooze
from his bones.

A flotilla of doves, willow-branch-laden, brush
his coiffed and perfumed head.
He enters a room of candelabra, of
massed candles, gold brocade, escorted by
two lutes, a zither, five violas.
A scurry of page-boys, lords and ladies,
suddenly stock-still, all
hushed for his passage.
In the frilled garb of half-naked choristers

two sopranos, a contralto
weave their voices towards some inner spring.
On a star-painted floor of darkness
two actors, their bodies draped in silk,
mime the fifteen poses of the sacred lovers.
In vestibules to right and left flutter
the red fleur-de-lis of Florence.
High horns float gold ripples of La Serenissima.
The centre aisle becomes the Grand Canal
as, across mirroring conflicted waters,
embroidered notes and coins sail back and forth
while, to each side, stone, metal, glass
press downward into earth.
From elaborate doorframes
pre-fabricated word-skeins glitter
a thousand ideograms for "Welcome."
All breath extols this
geography of love to which the lutes ascend.

Meanwhile the conference of skeletons by moonlight has
    begun.
L'Amoroso enters the chamber of x-rays
where everything inside him
is outside him, ribs and tubing, twirled
spirals of the ear, the listening
purple flora of the gut.
And beyond that lies the room of darkness
where only the eyes, nose and mouth
glow green and pink beyond
the steady mist of gathering black.

Stripped of his entourage
he wades in. Tall and elegantly gaunt,
a trawler in the velvet cape of a young prince,
he skims the waters of this psychic reservoir,
his body a net
loosely woven to fit the heart's detritus,
while his curled magician's sandals
stride the flood.

There is a cupboard known only
to the fish who are reborn each day from
the saint's recurrent nightmare of earth's death.
In this cupboard lie the dreams
L'Amoroso must invent:
the mountain that became a moon-struck eagle;
his days in the tabernacle of fire; his life
among the white stone trees, the white flowers,
a snowscape where his face is hidden
by the wind-dusted scree on
a lake's frozen surface.

And the cupboard opens its own several faces
as storage space for the afterlife of
broken computers, as the one darkness
where the skeletons won't go, or the mind's
inner signal box for lost trains,

while on a shelf L'Amoroso finds
a motel room that fits inside the palm of one hand
where over and over two lovers copulate

their mouths their genitals their souls
awaking each other into knowing
hour after hour for ever

and from the ream of notes for still-unwritten sonnets
tucked somewhere in the third drawer on the left
L'Amoroso's hand pulls out the phrase
"I must into the vale of Avalon
to heal me of my grievous wound."

2.

Tucked under the door to my apartment
a note on florid parchment:

> << *Por favor la sua presencia*
> *está invitado*
> *al gran concurso de los esqueletos*
> *afin que podía*
> *cenare conmigo ese notte*
> *El señor L'Amoroso.*>>

and straightaway I am transported
under earth, down caverns, through forests,
hurried by palanquin across tottering gorges,
halted on a bridge below a waterfall.
A fine mist passes through me
as I rise to stand at last
at one with the sky.

Meanwhile at my back I hear
the whirlwind of skeletons approach.
A chaos of air swirls overhead
and I step into
the altered hall of endings. Venice. 1610.
The lords and ladies chatter, the banners are assembled.
The high horns blazon
while outside on the runway
el señor L'Amoroso taxies in.

INVOCATIONS

Just look at you.
You're not that gypsy guy
the blonde without brakes ran into
on page 349 of the second volume.
Your squadron of necks is all a mess.
You arrive in a flotilla of disgraces.
At least you're not trying to run a brothel with no cash.
At least your confused head
points in the same direction as your gibbering kidneys.
When I ask for a one-word explanation
of our waning intimacy
the whole history of the Achmaenid Dynasty
betrayed by its subjects, battered by circumstance,
oozes up from your eyes, along with
Cyrus' palace torched by that brat Alexander
and enough cuneiform inscriptions
to rebuild China's Great Wall.
Incorruptible optimist re empathy.
Muddled devotee
condemned to the sacred prayer hall's outermost steps.
What is this road across the valley
where the horses of the king's guard
find pasture and sweet-smelling waters?

If I understood how to live in the arrow-point of the present
my breath would not darken this world.

PRINCE MYSHKIN, FALLING INTO DEEP SAMADHI BY THE STABBED BODY OF NATASHA FILIPOVNA, AWAKES ON A SIDEWALK IN MEXICO CITY

1.

Not even a chance to say *'Kak pozhivaetya?'* or *'Dobry vecher'*
and always the clanging bell
between *dom* and doom, between dome
and home, casa and catastrophe – that
slight echo of an inward bell.
From the highest mountains that I know
(intellectually) are there
From the pit of the low lake
that I understand in my bones
I am walking across
blocked and silted up and filled
with the ash of the dead
Again the skies blaze

Never before have I seen
Never before have I smelt
Never tasted
what the throat is flooded with

Here where over and over
road intersects road
is the true shape of the cross

In Switzerland where
in tall grass above the village
I lay held by the sky
In Russia where
snow melted into my eyes and all
was a vast work of fiction played out too fast

but here at the junction of all worlds
the feeling that, sooner or later,
the sky comes to an end
knowing my mind has become
a depot for abandoned umbrellas
and so, like that, should I set out?

Arriving in the land of fire
drawn into the immense bab-el
where my speech is the howl of the other side
not me not me
but the ones that made me
sky-shapers

Above the lake
above the burning
the house that is shining arises
fivefold dwelling place of all holy ones
and from windows of light
graceful arms lean out
hands joined in prayer
above the lake that is fire
above the doom that arrives from the four directions

above the collapsing causeway
in compassionate stillness

on the sidewalk the blare of a city
workmen demolishing whole blocks of humanity
gourd-carvers knife-grinders hat-hawkers taxi cabs fruit stalls

and already stepping out of the crowd
a young boy approaches me
bearing a letter held high in his time-frozen hand
and my hand has almost reached his
the letter has almost brushed the back of my hand
when a vision intervenes – a temple
that takes the place of a letter –
the sound of chanting
a junction of five dusty tracks under a banyan tree
a fivefold path

It is the night of unbearable brightness
My eyes utter blessings

2.

Dear Prince,

please forgive me,
It was I who wrote the letter
summoning you back from Switzerland,
I bribed two of those men

to share your railway carriage
and, all those times at the stations,
that face in the crowd you kept seeing was me.
I used you. I set you up.
It's true I was sent to Siberia,
was nearly shot by firing squad, nearly went mad,
but what I did interfering with your life
I know Christ will never forgive.
If I had left you in Switzerland
you would have grown strong with the children,
would have converted your irrepressible crowds of believers
in the riper cantons of Switzerland,
so much purer than us, so much closer to the sky.
I can foresee that in the war that is coming
you or your followers
would have converted to the peaceful joy of non-violence
that embittered man, the demagogue exile whose return
would bring so much suffering, so many deaths
to our Holy Mother Russia.
I know, then, through this one act on my part,
this whim, this caprice, the entire blood-soaked
misery of the 20th Century falls on my head.
But, even should I close my eyes to this,
that I brought you back,
that I bribed those men to entangle you,
that I made you meet Natasha Filipovna,
that I contrived for the beautiful Aglaia to fix her
somewhat bewildered need for conventional happiness on you:
all this is my unpardonable fault.

Maybe every life is like mine.
Maybe every life has so much guilt
it outstrips us,
a shame so large
there can never be room for the saying.
Maybe that is why we have ghosts,
those detached portions of uncontainable guilt
that go on trying to speak.

And now I have no idea where you are.
You never arrived back in Switzerland – I know that much.
So I have summoned the young boy with the faraway eyes,
have folded and sealed this letter, entrust it to him,
to his knowledge of all realms,
and (why even now do the words of another enter me,
why do I steal yet again from the future?)
send it a thousand miles thinking.

Yours in the love of God,

Fyodor Dostoyevski.

BRIEF FOOTNOTE

For some time I had been supervising at a distance the publication of a group of poems by Lazlo in an English magazine. I was concerned that at the last minute they would evaporate off the page, so slight was that Bulgarian Mexican's grip on reality. I could understand Mr Todorov's need to write under another name. I remember, several years back, a friend sent me a link to a blog where a young woman had just published one of my poems and one of her friends had posted: "I've always loved Peter Boyle. Everybody Loves Raymond is my favourite programme. I never knew he wrote poetry." I wanted to write to say I am not Peter Boyle the American actor, but was I sure? By then he had been dead several years but he seemed much more alive than me. Perhaps in some way I was him, lingering on under his name, slowly acquiring his face now he was gone. Perhaps I had always been his amanuensis. How can anyone know that someone else isn't writing them? And I thought: maybe all the dead have the same name.

ANTONIO ALMEIDA
(1899 – 1981)

Antonio Almeida was born in Ronda, Spain, in 1899. His father was an employee of the Hotel Reina Victoria but died when Antonio was still young. The family then moved to Valladolid where his mother's family lived. After working as a secretary to a local lawyer, Antonio settled in Madrid in 1934. In 1940 he migrated to Uruguay where he married. Following the military coup in Uruguay he settled with his daughter and son-in-law in Italy. He died in Rome in 1981.

He began writing poetry only late in life and a small selection was published in a Spanish-Italian edition by Pascoli Editores in Milan in 2001.

SELECTED POEMS

WAITING

I have sat down to listen to you.
I have drawn myself up into silence.
I have laid bare an imaginary table before me,
on a shelf beside me have placed two glasses –
a thimble of brandy, a wide cup of spiced tea –
and I have asked that you come
and I will listen.

It is night and cold
and I have searched so long for your presence,
your small voice in the large house
where all is absence.
Whatever you will say will find me out
housed as you are
on the outside of the world.

You are the one who lingers behind
in spaces vast and small
that wrap around the simplest things,
in ditches and lost jars,
in a row of streetlamps going nowhere,
in containers where the childhood of the dead
goes on trading bottle tops and cards.

And, if not you, who
will find for me in some forest depths
the fallen tree
where all walking stops?
A thousand white flowers
line the path through the sky.
So many have travelled that way

but you alone turned back from the door.
It is your voice I am waiting for.
Inside whatever words you say
in whatever language
it is your voice,
your being here still

in this world.

(TRANSLATED 10 AUGUST 2015)

TO PLACE THE DAWN AGAINST THE EYES
OF DARKNESS

To place the dawn against the eyes of darkness.
What we see through darkness,
what darkness sees through us.
Inside us every bone and every nerve
runs through darkness
and our eyes lift like heavy pebbles
to the surface of the light-world,
our whole being behind them.

(TRANSLATED 3 AUGUST 2015)

THE SECOND WORD OF INFINITY'S OTHER NAME OVERHEARD BY A YOUNG WOMAN CROSSING THE INTERSECTION OF MALDONADO AND PARAGUAY

You grow at the centre of my palm
as a speck where two lines meet
as you grow in the dawn ice glittering under a streetlamp
and in the stare of a startled cat
caught by a sweeper's broom behind rubbish bins.
You enter me from an open window
of a club where men are playing chess
or from a lone drop of rain
that brushes my left eye.
A driver adjusts his mirror.
A woman on an early morning bus
reapplies her lipstick.
Gently you take shape
like two letters on a kiosk's newspaper banner
marrying for the first time
with a steady indrawn breath
unheard in any human language
or you click behind me all at once
as the faint shudder of sound
that stumbles out of a dream fragment
to reappear as a car brakes.

My heart is light
as I walk with this chip of infinite mystery

rushing to the place where I must be
this morning.

(TRANSLATED 29 AUGUST 2014)

JULY EVENING

The girls are tying the prayer flags round the tree.
The flags are pinned at just beyond the height of
their heads. It is winter darkness where
they sit now and, by the older girl's shoulder,
two candles on a rock offer an orange glow.
The cold earth like the soft light
is temporary.

The mother and the father have stayed indoors
to look, settled at the table in the warm house,
while in the mother's hand in and out
a thread passes, mending a winter jacket.
Soon the girls will come back inside, soon
there will be tea and warm bread
and vegetables steamed in woven baskets
on the stove-top.

(TRANSLATED 12 JULY 2014)

ON MY FORTY-SECOND BIRTHDAY I TAKE THE BUS TO WORK

The world hangs off the edge
of a vast shelf tacked onto the void –
each time I close my eyes
it glitters faintly:
the eyes of ending.

Is there an answer in my hat
cocked at this angle among the hatless?
Will it save me
from all the terrors that lie
now half ahead and half behind me
dangling as I am
at the midpoint of my life?

You gather me, O Lord,
among those held
in the brief light.
For now you hold me back
from the great unmaking.

(TRANSLATED 15 AUGUST 2011)

THOUGHTS IN A CAFÉ

Day and world on a road that leads beyond.
I pass them by
and it's good to know
sparks left behind have lodged
in the leaves of the chinaberry tree
I saw in a photograph of a Cuban sidewalk, circa 1912.

Nothing is lost.
Sitting beside a mirror that runs
the whole length of this café
I wait at the very edge
of a double life. Every person,
every table, cup and plate
persists in its glassy being
and the tree outside, the buildings of the street
swim towards me, ignorant of death.
Men and women lean into each other,
stand or drift. The stillness
of a Sunday without end
muffles their voices. We have
all the time of that unmoving cloud resting
above the shoulder of the young girl
with her far-away smile and long long ponytail.

My eyes lift to see your face
on the threshold of the corridor that descends,
goes on descending through

the mind's still centre:

gone   gone   utterly gone.

(TRANSLATED 12 DECEMBER 2010)

KNOWINGS

What voice is
at the bottom of that path
as it turns and turns

like the dropped stone
that from the darkness
knows already

the sound that
will echo from
the well's stillness:

the ripple
it always held
in itself.

*

So little time to weave the fabric together,
thread after thread
unpicking me into no one.

*

On the shopping list of things unwanted but inevitable
I have written "grief" –
it's there on every shelf in every store,

on the labels hidden under the labels
and the world seems to know
you will always need more of this.

*

Ice floes surround me
like lost children.
My head in and out of water

cresting for a home, myself
as I will be,
bent by some

cosmic curvature
a blip of air.

(TRANSLATED 18-22 AUGUST 2007)

RAIN AT DAWN

We are waiting for the plane
as first light comes through the eerie terminal
and the boom of voices dies out.

Back home in a neighbour's garden the jasmine
have just opened their overpowering fragrance
and already the rain is shredding their white puffs
here and there.

In black suits holding black bundles
we are waiting for the plane
and not all of us will make it
to the other shore.

(TRANSLATED 19 SEPTEMBER 2001)

THE TIME OF WEEPING

When I could walk no more
I lay down at the side of the road,
beaten down, curled up,
my head wrapped in my arms.

A man went by who wept for his lost fortune.
Then a man passed by weeping for his lost home

and then another who wept for his lost father
and then, bathed in the same dust, a man
came weeping, the shape of his lost child
draped over his shoulders.

A man came staggering but almost upright,
his lost family strapped to his back.
His weeping was no longer of this earth
but tore at the sky.

And then a man approached slowly,
carrying the weight of his lost family
and a million more brothers and sisters murdered beside them.
His weeping had lost its tears.
His weeping was a rip that ran
from the crown of his head
to the fingertips of his right hand.

And then came a man
who carried on his back every face that had once
been like his face, every look, every human gesture
and all the beings of the earth and the inhabitants of the sky
that had perished as well.
His weeping was quiet, almost silent,
and he wept that his weeping
should be the last human sound.

And I got up and took up my walking stick
and I made a very small sign in the dirt by the side of the road
that here was the end
to my time of weeping.

(TRANSLATED SEPTEMBER 1997)

LYING UNDER A BEE-SWARM

1.
Before it rots inside us,
before it becomes the insatiable wasps
devouring us from the inside,
the underworld is first the immensity of light in our hands.

2.
This buzzing that won't go away from the centre of your head:
let it fill you like all of summer
in the long afternoon that is your life.

3.
What these whisper-gods have whispered
holds the inflection of an earth-language
that burrows down into you
as into the soil that is also you.

4.
What you dreamed of then:
to create citadels of sunlight,
to create black and gold
banners of arrival.

5.
Open this envelope of honey with your teeth,
in the corners of your tongue
read the underside of sweetness.

6.
Life-skeins, larger even than
the breath exhaled towards the faint speck of winter sun,
like the honeycomb of ice on a window,
one long line of almost-words
each crafted in gold.

(TRANSLATED DECEMBER 1993 - MARCH 1994)

THE TALL HOUSE BY THE RAVINE

The window of the forsaken is here.
You can climb so high but no higher.
And when they come looking for you
it's no use trying to wander off.
The unmistakeable scent
of your way of thinking this world
will always give you away –
or the afterglow left
by that persistent ache in your spine
or those irregular burrowing marks
dug in the soil by your limp.
Even when you are blind
a leakage of the light trapped in your eyes
leaves that scent of having nowhere to go.

Impossible to come back now.
This cloister is your empty tomb
that you carry with you
the way the thoughts of snails
build this vast shell of silence
over them.

And yet and yet
in this window in this house
at the edge of the final cliff
your eyes can't let go of the sky.

(TRANSLATED JUNE-SEPTEMBER 1985)

CONVERSATION WHILE WAITING

Who has gone furthest away from me?

Is the sky to be trusted
and, when I die,
will my feet point left or right?

It is night now
and the trucks delivering forgiveness
and frozen fiestas
have still not arrived.

Can the hidden alphabet
be made plain?

A few steps beyond the deserted esplanade
light and the reassuring hum
of distant planets vanish.
Far from me
the waves withdraw, muttering
an unknown language of intimate collapse.

I am waiting to enter
the rollcall of their
magnificent thunder.

(TRANSLATED MAY 1984 – 3 DECEMBER 2015)

EXCERPTS FROM ANTONIO ALMEIDA'S
SKETCH FOR A BIOGRAPHY

I had never really seen my own city – who does? – until
those two or three weeks when I guided the foreigner, the
poet, here or there, to see this or that place, to purchase
little gifts he wanted for friends in Austria or Germany or
Paris. It was December 1912 and I was thirteen years old.
But, before I tell the story of myself and the poet, I must
say a little about myself as I was then. The fourth child
in a family of six, I stuttered a lot and was very slow of
speech, often withdrawing for days into complete silence. It
had – I was told – something to do with an illness I had as
an infant. Some of the local boys teased me but there was
a group who stood by me, accepting me as I was. I knew
myself that, though blocked from words, I wasn't stupid. My
father always believed in me. When a famous poet came to
stay at the hotel where he worked, my father decided being
around someone so different might help. A curandera had
told him the angels had touched me and, if I met the right
person, I would start to find my own way into speech. It
was my father's idea to suggest me as the poet's unofficial
local assistant. I was an odd choice to guide a poet, and yet
we communicated easily, rapidly in our mostly wordless
way. He was always writing in his notebook or on sheets of
Hotel paper – letters often, I knew that, but sometimes just
notes or lines of poems he would repeat aloud in his slightly
ringing, harsh, bright German, to see how they sounded.
I think he needed to walk in order to see, in order to help

his breath find the flow of words. Some mornings he read a book as he walked – from its cover I saw it was the Koran.

I remember one day especially. We had walked to the southern edge of the city, to visit my Aunty's workshop where she made tiny mosaics of glass. He'd just bought one as a souvenir when we began the walk back. There was a large barren patch between two houses. "Look," he said, and I turned in the direction I thought he was pointing. How this could be I don't know, but there was a lion resting against a wall and an old man with a very long beard at its feet. In the man's lap a book was open. Its binding was the colour of blood, the colour of flames. The lion looked right into me, peacefully, like the gentlest possible summons or like an offering. In a moment the vision vanished: just thistles, barren space, pale cold winter light against a whitewashed wall. Then the poet said again, "Don't you see it?" and I realised he had been pointing in a different direction, not at that small barren patch, but at an immense stretch of land and sky over which there was a rainbow.

Only much later, when I wrote down this vision, did I understand it enough to question: was it meant for the poet, but he was looking the wrong way? Was it meant for me, but I was only thirteen, almost wordless and would not write poetry for another thirty years? Some time later I first saw a painting of Saint Jerome. The man in my vision was similar to him, but not the same. The man I saw was older and belonged to a world far more ancient, far more of this earth and beyond this earth, than Christianity. In any case, it wasn't the old man who looked deeply into me, but the lion. I have since thought that, maybe, the lion was one of those powerful angels who come to earth at various times.

When the poet – Rilke as I later learnt – left early the next year, the memory of those days, those images, stayed with me. From then on poetry and its connection to a world other than this, a world that erupts into this, was something always there in the back of my consciousness.

My father died when I was seventeen and my mother moved us to Valladolid where her older brother lived. There I worked as a secretary for a lawyer, wrote and filed correspondence and arranged his appointments. In April 1922, just before my twenty-third birthday, he sent me for a week to Madrid with a series of errands to attend to. I took an afternoon train that was due to reach Madrid around midnight. As it wound slowly through the Guadarrama, about half-way through the journey, the train stopped at Segovia to let on new passengers. In my compartment there was now a young woman with a child, a disturbed looking man of about forty and a man whose age and occupation I at first found hard to judge but, since he read and wrote the entire trip, I quickly dubbed him "the professor." The small boy was soon asleep in the woman's lap. The middle-aged man began mumbling to himself and gazed anxiously at the window as if some disaster was pressing on him and he didn't know how to lift it. I was travelling light, my battered case containing only the few items of clothing and toiletries needed for a week in the capital. I could sense that, though the "professor" appeared fully absorbed in his own papers, he was taking in everything around him, sifting and holding clear the essence of everyone in that small compartment. At some point I began to think of him not as "the professor" but as "the poet."

About an hour out of Madrid rain started falling. We seemed at once strangely isolated, the inhabitants of a tiny ark labouring through the mountains and the darkness. It felt, that night, as if a great catastrophe was heading towards all of us, but also I sensed that something powerful was protecting us. I imagined an invisible rainbow had haloed our train. Eventually we reached Madrid. On the platform two or three people were there to greet the man I thought of by now as "the poet" and so I overheard his name: Antonio Machado. As happens when you are young and such things mean more, I was struck by the coincidence of our names: Antonio, Saint Anthony, the patron saint of finding.

Several years later I bought the book *Nuevas canciones* and saw the poem "Iris de la noche." Instantly I recognised the woman, the small boy falling asleep in her lap, the anxious man mumbling to himself. I was not, am not, in the poem. You might imagine that this would have disappointed me but not at all. I understood I was not in the poem because, like Machado, I was a witness to the miracle that takes place in the poem and so, of necessity, must be outside it. I had seen those people, our small compartment surrounded by night, in the way Machado had seen it, had written it inwardly without words and so was being marked as a poet without yet being able to write poems. I felt Machado had left me out to tell me what matters most: "The poet is outside the frame. He preserves the needed balance by extinguishing himself. Instead of being buffeted by the chaotic, disordered back and forth of feelings, instead of sinking secret hooks into others by proclaiming what we take to be our own love or tenderness, the poet needs selflessness. Only in that way can the feelings that things generate in themselves be perceived most powerfully, be taken somewhere inside ourselves to find, eventually, their true words."

But, for all that, in the following twenty years, though I tried several times, there were no poems. I remained wordless and alone in life. In July 1936 when the war broke out I joined the Republican Army. Working with others, swept up in the struggle, I started to lose my wordlessness. Wounded at Teruel, I was moved to the Communications section first in Madrid, then in Barcelona. In the end I made it across the frontier into France and there met Ana Mercedes, Emilia's mother. We married on the boat to Uruguay and, along with so many other Spanish refugees, began our new life in Montevideo. Not long after the birth of Emilia I started to write the first poems that I felt worked as poems. It was extremely slow, requiring endless revisions, and at first I only wrote one poem every two or three years, but poems I was willing to accept did at last start to come.

I was now a successful businessman, owner of a small electrical supplies and repairs shop. Life seemed settled when my wife, Ana Mercedes, fell ill with an extreme fever and, without the doctors ever diagnosing what it was, died in the course of three terrifying days. I was in a state of shock and despair. I did not know how I would find the strength to continue. I had a fourteen-year-old daughter to take care of but I could barely take care of myself. My life felt as if it had been completely torn out of me. It was in this state that I met the man whom I still think of as Elijah.

About a month after Ana Mercedes' death, night came down within me. I felt the absolute certainty that, for the moment, I must place my daughter apart from me, somewhere safe. We had neighbours who were very kind and so I left my daughter with them and walked out into night. Soon I had no sense of where I had walked or who I was. In front of me and behind me streets elongated or changed shape. For the first time the weight of everything I had lived through – my father's death, the loss of my family in the Civil War, the crushing of Spain, and now Ana Mercedes' death – jolted me like a massive explosion of wiring in the chest, like a heavy blow to my temples. I walked and walked. How many hours had gone by? I remember seeing a bridge over railway tracks and the line of the sea.

I was seated on a bench when I returned to myself. From the dampness of my face I knew I had been weeping. I still did not know where I was or how I might find my way back. I could grasp little more than the memory of my name, "Antonio," and the image of my daughter. I remembered she was safe with the neighbours if I could only remember where I lived.

In this darkness that seemed beyond darkness a tall man with a rough beard and dirty clothes appeared, someone with the looks of those who live on the street, "un clochard," the French word came to me I don't know why. I don't know how to say this but he looked completely through me, a brusque, almost contemptuous look that mingled with an extraordinary delicacy. "I have been sent to bring you home," he announced. I was confused by his strange statement and started asking a string of questions. He just looked at me with a sort of condescending impatience that, in other circumstances, might have angered me. "I am here. That's enough," he replied. Then through a series of questions, word by word, he prompted me to remember my surname, my occupation, the name of where I worked, the cafés I went to, my daughter's name. Memory came more easily because it felt that he knew all these things already and was only pretending curiosity to help me fix these things more clearly in my mind.

So we began our walk back, but it was not a straight walk. I was soon aware he was guiding me a very long way around past various shops that sold pastries, past a synagogue, a barber's shop, a chess club. From time to time people greeted him in Yiddish. And all the while we talked – or, to be more precise, he talked and I listened. He knew everything that I knew but much more. He recited in German the poems Rilke had written in Ronda and the poem by Machado. He spoke of the madness in Europe and in Spain. Most of all we talked – how this happened I don't know – of the book of Job. He would take a few lines of Job and interpret them one way, then demolish what he had said and interpret them another way. I cannot remember the details of his arguments but, as his commentary went backwards and forwards across the book, I felt the history of humanity and my own history were held there, acted out and made clear in his words. As we traced our way back in slowly narrowing circles I could feel Job's anger, his knowledge of himself and his determination not to let God off, cleansing me. At one moment, like a sudden jolt, like a voice both inside and outside me, I heard the words, "Write the poems. Write all the poems." How my poems could be connected to the story of Job I don't know but it felt clear, that night, that they were. More quietly, but several times, a sentence also slipped into my head: "You have your daughter and your poems – that is your lighted path through the wilderness." Three times I heard that sentence though I am sure neither myself nor the stranger said those words.

Just after dawn I stood on the landing outside the neighbour's apartment and rang the buzzer. As I heard someone come to the door I glanced around but he had gone already. I thanked the neighbour and went back to my flat with my daughter. By now there was a strong sense of calm in me, enough to focus on the tasks ahead. About two years later my daughter made friends with a girl who had recently lost her father. The mother and I never quite worked out to be a couple, but there was a beautiful July evening I remember when all four of us stayed at a place she owned in the country. I remember the girls wanting to mark the evening by tying prayer flags round the tree.

Several years went by. I had been working late one evening at the repair shop when a boy arrived with a note he said had been given him by a strange man who looked like a hobo. The note asked me to meet him at a certain intersection not far away in an hour's time. I knew it must be the man I still thought of as Elijah. Sure enough there he was at the intersection. He told me that things would get bad in this country very soon and, when they did, I should take my family elsewhere. He said I should go to Italy and gave me the names and addresses of people who could help me there. When I asked for his name he smiled and said, "Just describe me. They will know who I am." He took an envelope from his raincoat and gave it to me. "I don't need this," he said, "but it will help you buy the four plane tickets you will need. Don't wait too long – the moment the violence starts to happen, go." Five years later what he said came true – the military dictatorship, death squads. And by then he was right – there were four of us as my daughter was now married with a son and also a baby, a daughter, who travelled with her and didn't need a ticket.

How I came to meet Antonio Almeida: Rome airport, March 1981.

At the end of August 1980 I went to Madrid, intending to spend at least a year there teaching English and learning Spanish. As it happened I was there little more than six months, my plans overtaken by the onset of depression and a series of anxiety attacks that convinced me I had to return to familiar surroundings. It was with a profound sense of defeat, of repeated failure, that I set about organising my return.

Although I had originally thought of flying home through London, I found a cheaper deal that involved flying to Rome and spending a few days there before flying on to Sydney. I had barely collected my baggage and entered the main concourse of Rome airport when a woman approached me. She spoke to me in Spanish and asked a strange series of questions: "Did I speak Spanish? Had I come from Madrid? Was I Irish?" (I told her I was Australian but my ancestors came from Ireland – "That's perfect," she said.) "Was I a poet?" (To which I answered "Yes" though, at that time, I had written very few poems.) She then introduced herself as

Emilia and explained briefly that she wanted me to meet her father who was very ill and had been looking for someone who matched my description – my limp, my age, my Irish background, my coming on a flight at that hour from Spain – to entrust the eventual translation of his poems to. I gathered they were following some kind of prediction, possibly an act of cartomancy, and that, to them, knowledge of the Spanish language, something that could always grow over time, was less important in their translator than an obsession with poetry. ("However long you require, whatever you can manage, even just five or six poems. You have many years ahead of you. Think of it as a blessing for both of us," Antonio said.)

I at once went with her, like a sleepwalker guided by forces to which he has completely surrendered. Emilia drove me to the hospital where her father was, then later I stayed at her place, along with her husband and two children. I felt entirely safe in their presence as if all the fears I had been through myself were now at an end, or at least as if, through her, I had been given a sign that this darkness in my life now had a term set to it. By becoming her father's translator I had been given a fresh chance at life.

THE MONTAIGNE POET

New Essays by Montaigne
(published in Paris and Barcelona, 2003)

THE MONTAIGNE POET

In 2003 *The New Essays of Montaigne* was published. The *prière d'insérer* of the French edition identified the author as "The Montaigne poet" while the simultaneous Spanish edition gave the same name to its author on the front and back covers.

Beyond the obvious fun of transparent hoaxing, *The New Essays of Montaigne* draws attention to two distinctively French literary forms – the essay as developed by Michel de Montaigne in the late 16th Century, and the prose poem initiated by Aloysius de Bertrand, Baudelaire and Rimbaud in the 19th Century but gaining its full prominence in the 20th Century with such masters of the form as Francis Ponge, Max Jacob, Henri Michaux and René Char. *The New Essays* perhaps suggests a convergence between the two traditions – both open forms enabling the inclusion of all sorts of material previously considered "non-literary," both inviting rapid transformations and reflections on the most varied issues, both capable of being either very personal or almost impersonal in their examination of a topic from multiple sides.

My selection here is no more than a taster. I have chosen a mix of those prose poems, verse poems or essays dealing with personal life, including the life of one working inside a bureaucracy (a parallel, after all, to Montaigne's reflections on service to the state) alongside others that reflect on writing itself (again a major theme of Montaigne's work).

The reader will find some further discussion of the publication and reception of the work in a Postscript after the poems.

THE MONTAIGNE POET: SELECTED POEMS AND MICRO-ESSAYS

ON FALLS: BY WAY OF A PREFACE

Concussed I see a strange man sitting opposite me, in ruffled lace and black doublet. He is speaking to me in Latin. He has just fallen off a horse as I have just fallen from a height when a balustrade gave way. Our death is so close to both of us that if we stretched out our fingers the same ice would form along their edges, extending their tips until they meet. It is the year 1995 – it is the year 1575. I am listening to him: his voice enters me. As I wake from the operation to fix my shattered legs and my left shoulder blade he gives me my instructions: "Write."

OF BLINDNESS AND GOD'S IMMEDIACY

He folded and turned the paper, mumbling to himself and rocking in the one space of thin white light before the wall. Later they placed the folded paper, along with all the others, on a bent iron plate and slid it into the oven. And then the oven stopped. They pulled it out and unfolded the strangely shaped paper. There was no writing on it. He did not know how to write. The twists and kinks of the paper were his mnemonic — his way of impressing his story on the world because, from birth, he could not speak. And that is why the oven went out: there was no need for his paper to be burnt — it had already been directly read by God.

Immediately they went to find him in the vast underground prison that, in those days, was all that was left of their lives. They looked everywhere but neither he nor his body was found. The suggestion was then made (no one remembers now who said it) that he must have been taken up painlessly, breathlessly, in a single act of translation into the other world.

OF HOW COMFORTABLY AT HOME ONE
MAY FEEL, EVEN WHEN LEFT OUTSIDE

I am not an elephant though I could have been one. The savannah is where I feel most at home, but especially the moment when I descend into the river's rippling transparency. My back sprayed with water, my eyes weeping with the joy of it. I have in my time been equally a victim and a trampler but, all in all, far more of my time has been spent drawing the folds of the world around me. I once visited a small city and, peering into the glass enclosure that confined them, watched a group of young humans slowly employing their fingers to stuff wedges of potato into their mouths. Entirely absorbed in the fragrance and the salt of it. I could well understand and admire their ability to ward off ageing and anxiety with mechanical self-comforting motions. The great boneyard will be ours soon enough.

ON THE QUEST FOR GOOD GOVERNANCE

The boy rode the bicycle. Attached to it by numerous strings and a sturdy silver chain rolled the great multi-dimensional, many-roomed structure sometimes called "The Palace," sometimes "The House of Oversight." This contorted building is remarkable for having no windows on any of its surfaces. Its walls are jutted and curved with many turrets and convoluted stove-pipe formations, with protruding barn-like appendages, the whole a brownish red or reddish brown in the morning, a subdued grey at midday, somber violet by nightfall. Many have claimed it is in fact colourless, merely reflecting the different shadings of light in the changing environments through which it moves.

The young boy riding the bicycle that drags this immense structure from land to land is selected from the nine year olds of a certain mountainous kingdom. Removed from his family, for two years he receives intense training in the arts of bicycle riding. He will then be solemnly enthroned as the rider, a position of both awe and slight denigration that never lasts beyond his sixteenth birthday. Even after only six months he is exhausted far beyond his years, drained by the psychic stress of pulling such a weight of universal implication behind him. Every few years a new rider must be chosen. The reasons for these procedures are, like so much else concerning this moveable structure, endlessly debated. Some say it is because the rider must be fresh and optimistic, showing always a pleasant child-like face to the world. Others maintain it is to ward off the temptation to arrogance in the person of the young man who should, in truth, be regarded as the lowest servant, so the sayings go, not the prince-like intermediary, pedalling always towards some space between humanity and the gods. Others again claim it is simply the level of exhaustion and the risks of an accident that necessitate such frequent changes.

The first that anyone will see of the approaching "Staatsapparat," as the "Palace" or "House of Oversight" is sometimes known, is the boy on the bicycle. Quite some distance behind him, longer and longer distances over the millennia according to the varying chronicles of some historians, trundles the brown/grey/red/violet structure. It is parked in a town for a week or six months and, during that time, the governance of everything is turned upside down.

At its most obvious level the purpose of this moveable structure is to instruct all mankind in the correct forms of social contact, from how to wash dishes to the sowing of crops, from the shaving of a man's beard before death by strangulation or the plaiting of a grandmother's hair prior to the rite of live burial to the correct way to lace one's boots. Every profession and trade must be inspected and, where possible, overturned. No subject is too weighty or too trivial for intervention and improvement.

What happens inside the structure? What procedures are followed to arrive at their rulings? Should one imagine a giant library on wheels or rather a small kingdom with an endless array of viziers, elder statesmen and courtiers? And how is the light needed to see generated within there? On all these questions confused rumours abound. More will be said below on the question of purposes and procedures but first some comments on the means of illumination within the structure. Sparks of the great fire of origins have been preserved and remain burning faintly in alcove stands on every floor, along every corridor, according to the most common account. But perhaps it is simply that the eyes of those who live here have adjusted to a permanent murky greyness, a texture that is neither light nor darkness.

Purposes and procedures are always interlaced and the subject of the greatest disagreements. Some say there is a single elaborate, almost infinite book from before memories begin and it is from there, however fraught with the risk of errors in copying or transmission, that the rulings are drawn. Others seem quite sure there are no books at all, only a moveable concealed inner world of palace coups, rival cliques and ignorance. For what books or codices could they possibly consult in making such confusing pronouncements and how could anyone consult an infinite book in finite time? Certainly the rulings given by this so-called "state within all states" are often strange: a confused scramble at best, to judge from the often inconsistent and seemingly arbitrary judgments they pronounce. Others, of course, find the deepest wisdom and method in their rulings. To believe otherwise, the proverb goes, is like doubting the stars and the moon.

The look of extraordinary distaste when this structure's officials behold human difference, that crinkling of the nose before local customs or private inspiration, has been frequently observed when they first step through the portals of the moving citadel to inspect some new town or province. You can sense in their every word, their every glance, so our old folks say, a limitless horror of ordinary people developing their own solutions to life's perplexities. That and the terror that an individual might some day find one of the long-concealed paths that lead out of this already collapsing world.

ON TRANSLATING A LINE BY VIRGIL

ibant obscuri sola sub nocte per umbram

and dark they travelled under night's silent loneliness

marb murep et con bus a los iruscs o t nabi

and with searching for the Irusci so foolish seemed the nabi:
marred be your reputation
and with a bus may you erupt among nebulae

travelling obscurely solo sub nightscape
the bantu scurrilously ole oleing "up night"
night bus to the Jerusalem hot tubs
with a bat darkly solitude city of night

the wedding of the Dioscuri
took place in a submarine
we the witnesses
trailing moist feathers through night

OF THE SPACE BELOW A DOOR

Two women are speaking softly
in a language I don't understand
and pointing at a long strip of sunlight
coming in under the door.
I do not know what sort of thing people could talk about,
pointing at sunlight coming in
under a door.
Their voices are a soft concerned accompaniment
to whatever is going on in this world.
Whether familiarity or wonder prompts them,
or something else I've entirely overlooked,
all hangs for now
in the perfect, infinitely open moment
of not knowing.
Is this what God is like?

OF PARENTS AND CHILDREN

At any age one can need adoption. Equally at any age one can yearn to have a child of one's own. And why not both at the same time? A person puts their name down in the queue to adopt and, simultaneously, in another queue to be adopted. (They may have children who have grown up; they may have parents who have died; whatever.) They wait for years and years, they wait their whole lifetime. Suns rise and set on this double unattainable craving. They think: what is it to have lived without having parents? What is it to have lived without being a parent? They feel like the shell of some strange creature that has swallowed its own beginning and its end. I cannot imagine what it means to have never had a parent or to live without a child since I grew up with parents and have had children of my own. And yet those who wait forever to adopt and be adopted are also us as we are at every moment: profoundly, inextricably alone.

OF HOW IT IS AND IS NOT TRUE THAT THIS FOLLOWS THAT

That moment when you realise that if you walk along the narrow footpath pressed up against the blue walls using your hands to move yourself like a mountaineer between parked cars and the sheer drop of sky blue wall, if you advance that way down the empty tangle of curving back streets in this foreign town under a blazing midday sun that in any case doesn't reach these narrow lanes, moving spread-eagled in spaces that expand, vertiginous and vertical in a world that could go on for ever, if you start like that and continue as you start, there is no reason to believe any of the days you lived up to that moment ever existed. Your whole life begins anew on the blue walls of this town, yourself a bewildered fly pasted forever to a single infinite surface. As the wall curves with unimaginable slowness towards a gradual bend, the blueness overwhelms. No reason, you say, to think I ever was.

ON READING A BOOK

"There remained for him," he began to read in the book as he turned the page but suddenly, in that moment, there were no longer words but, where it might have said sunset, there was the immense stretch of sky gone red and purple at the edges in that far away city where he was ten years old and his father with a look bordering on some long repressed despair said, "I hate sunsets - they always make me feel sad, and in this place at this time of year the sunsets last for hours," and he tried to understand the strangeness of his father and looked into the sunset that, at that instant, seemed to him only time and he didn't yet understand how it also had the final taste of sadness, and next there was sunrise, the long pink sky from an upstairs window and birds that could be heard everywhere but never seen, and as if rising from a deep sea, complete with the clanging of a bell from its green and yellow tram, breath rising from the mouths of four or five travellers, all muted, hands moving out of pockets as they reached for the bar to swing themselves up onto the running board, the road appeared in all its blackness with the two lines of silver track coated in a sheen of melted ice, and where it said "lead to" he was drawn bend after bend down the twin grey lines of the tracks, so he could feel his whole face taken over by forward motion, next trees were flickering at the edge of eyesight, a row of evergreens that approached one by one as the tram swung round another corner, the bay was there a rim of blueness, cold, unmoving at that hour in air that carried no breeze, that left no ripple in the water or his hair because it too was waiting to be touched, a wall was there next, cream-coloured, rough in texture, the stone rough-hewed with small swarming peaks and elevations on its surface, doors, three, four of them, red-brown, grey, red again, then cars a row of them, a kerb, next a bridge, under it the rush of a river entering the bay and he waited there, stranded a moment in the trembling of water far under him, the darkness ready to dissolve him, and as a first adjective approached, as he was driven into it as into a first wedge of sound that would coat the next object in colour, touch or weight, in fragrance, warmth or chill, dullness or radiance, he felt this could last, was already lasting, forever, while far ahead he sensed, not yet formed, but already weaving space's curvature in readiness for its own birth, a remote distance away, a lifetime away, the mystery of something the objects would never hold, something beyond them, incomprehensible to their steady presence, the jarring vertigo of the first full-stop.

ON FIRST WORDS BEST WORDS

Anyone could have written this poem. I say it to myself. Maybe I wrote this poem – or maybe a young girl who wants to feel what it's like to write a poem, or maybe an elderly man who wants to feel what it's like to be a young girl dreaming of writing a poem. The words are there and I have no idea of their value. Perhaps they will be the last poem I will write. The young girl leans her head above the page and sees a lotus pond and, at her back, a Buddhist temple, the big one on the hill overlooking the freeway – one she doesn't care for much anymore with its flashy bright red designs and excessive architecture, a kind of moneyed gesture, she guesses now, from some wealthy Taiwanese businessman wishing to acquire good karma, a kind of pre-emptive atonement. Is that what poems are, she hears herself wondering. There is so much goodness in her the world will never contain it. All evening, as she prepares to write, dense thunder is marshalling itself on the four horizons. When she got home from visiting her mother in the hospital she found a grasshopper in the kitchen and took it outside, trapping it in a large glass jar before releasing it on the veranda into the large pot with her grandmother's orchids. That and the long bamboo lounge-chair remind her of her grandmother, the legacy of a kindly deity around the house. How much goodness can she contain? Can goodness write a poem and, if not, why then write poems? This is no vanity, only (as with her meditation) the desire to go deeper. Because time is short. Because her whole long life is no more than the twenty minutes it takes for a storm to gather. Already lightning and heavy rain beat against the windows all around her. Her pen is there above the page. And she writes. Anyone could have written this poem.

Coda:

The girl has placed line breaks in the poem which the old man reading over her shoulder mentally takes out.
The line breaks have
no reason to be there – they
could as well be here
or here.
She has put them in
to say
this is a poem.
The older man thinks you can also show that this is a poem just by saying this is a poem. Leaving out line breaks is, to him, a more economical way of filling space. Why not just say read this slowly. A full stop is a kind of line break. Sort of. Maybe the girl is more visual
or the man more
aesthetically atrophied.
It matters little. Either way space is filled. And emptiness left.

Anyone could have written this poem.

ON THE LIMITS OF SELF-EXPRESSION

– You can't put your things on the table. It's part of the rules of this cruise ship.

– I didn't know I was on a cruise ship. I thought this was simply the earth, I thought we were anchored into it.

– No, the cruise ship is never the same as the earth. You can't see the sea, of course – that would be too obvious. You will see rocks and stones, the greenery of passage and the heavy mists of winter, they move past you and around you. But I say it again: you can't put your things on the table. All those sequences of words will have to go, and the long strings of rainbow-coloured beads you wanted to show others, it's not allowed. You can smear yourself in the colours of the earth if you wish – that's the nearest you can come to hinting at whatever it is you understand by that distasteful overused expression, "the journey."

OF SLEEP AND WAKING

I wake in the bed beside Marie in my parents' house. We are in the large room at the far end that had once been the stables, then a ballroom and later a dormitory for children orphaned during the religious wars and the decades of relatively benign chaotic violence that followed. Through the long bay window the grey night sky is a maze of clouds and small distant specks of brightness. At the other end of the room a closed door with a panel of misted glass leads to the long corridor, the other sleeping quarters and the rest of the house. Beyond that door nothing is visible, no presence of the night sky, no trace of anything to guide you from one space to another. The door's frosted surface masks the immeasurable distance of the fall into nowhere. Just before it, still in our room with its once glittering parquet floor, someone has left a small light burning. It is this light which has woken me. Should I get out of bed and extinguish it? But then would I too, the last of all the generations of my family, be engulfed in the same darkness? When I say these words have I already entered nowhere?

ON THE ETERNAL NATURE OF FRESH BEGINNINGS

This body next to you, said the German expert on design, is your ideal self – what you climbed out of once and have since forgotten about. Like gills and dialogues with rainbows, like your life as a ruminant quadruped, it has been erased from your waking story. When the time is right you will step inside it and it will transport you. Do not look at the claws that dangle from its withered right arm – consider only its wings. Say to yourself the word "Perfection." Be confident. All the stars of the universe were placed millennia ago far inside you.

OF ROOMS

—When you no longer have country there are only rooms.

A room exists only between walls.
It has nowhere else to go.
Seen from the street it is
an abstraction, mere guesswork.
From inside it opens outward:
an entire realm.
On first inspection a room
may resemble a narrow box.
It gains its space only
by being filled up.
A prisoner of normality
it witnesses birth, lovemaking and death
with an equal discrete reticence.
It holds its counsel as
a late-come codifier of
whatever may be the assemblages
and general booty of a life.
Breathe in that moment when
staleness and promise are one.
Touch the handle of the doorknob,
let it rest against your palm:
the crisp sensation
of one who exits or enters
brushed by an immense neutrality.
A door is to a room

as a butterfly is to a row of flowers
in late summer:
the flutter, the sudden
fragrance of
a resplendent elsewhere.
It is not for me to use the word "illusory."

OF BOOKS AND SILENCE

He is guiding me,
a man in a red fez,
beside what seems to be a line of bookcases
but what he holds in his hand is a long curved oar
with which he moves our flat-bottomed skiff forward
between the windows and spires, the winding façades of the
drowned city.

Yes, he says,
all the books of the earth are here,
including those that to you
are not yet written.
Your books are here too somewhere
though we have not come for them.
I want most of all for you to feel this place,
to have the sense that it is here
on the earth's other side.
When you wake
you will remember the feel of the water under you,
the freshness of the air
in this moment of always beginning
and these delicately tinted mirrors of glass that are books.
No one can read them all –
it is enough to drift between them
as we are doing.
The light that drips from them,
from the slightly ajar edges that are their pages,

is enough to guide you home.

– And the books, I ask,
what do they say?
Facing my last years of pain and my death,
what do they say?

– As we drift past, he says,
place your hand beside this row of light-blue windows
that are also books.
Now listen: do you understand?
The silence changes.

THE MONTAIGNE POET: A POSTSCRIPT

One of the minor literary scandals of the summer of 2003 was the simultaneous appearance in France and Spain of a slender volume purporting to be the channelled voice of Montaigne, as recorded in the séances of a group calling themselves "the last true surrealists" who met in certain cellars in Paris or Barcelona – a work published under the name of "the Montaigne poet." The Spanish edition stated on its cover that it was a translation from the French, the French that it was translated from the Spanish. No one ever claimed authorship of the book and the publishers in both countries stood by their agreement to preserve the anonymity of the purported author or authors. Several experts claimed that the French version was superior and undoubtedly the original, minor irregularities in tense formation confirming their opinion. However, two rival experts stated it was clearly originally written in Spanish. There were a few odd usages of words in the French, and the Spanish had, in general, a more lively tone. I have chosen to use the Spanish version – not because I believe it to be more authentic but because somehow it feels superior as poetry in Spanish. I might add that Jorge Zalameya's Spanish translation of Saint-John Perse's *Oiseaux* immediately felt to me more convincing, more satisfying as poetry than the French original. What in Perse's French sometimes seemed a too insistent straining for grandeur became in Spanish a natural, slightly erratic, flight above jagged landscapes.

In 2005 an article in *Le Monde* claimed to have solved the mystery. The author was not one but two people: identical twins, one living in Auteuil, the other in Valladolid, children of Spanish immigrants from the 1950s. The twin sisters wrote alternate sentences of each essay: the one in Auteuil in French, the one in Valladolid in Spanish. When a poem was finished each would take responsibility for preparing the version in one language only. Over the course of several years they completed the book and then talked the publishers in Paris and Barcelona into simultaneous anonymous publication. The only trouble with this theory was that no one ever found the twins. An attempt was made by one journalist to track down the money trail: where did the royalty cheques go? An account number was found for a bank in Nancy as well as a branch of the Banco de Bilbao on Gran Via in Madrid. Both accounts had by then been closed: the one in Nancy was in the name of Michel Eyquem, the one in Madrid in Marie de Gournay's name: another dead-end. There had long been the suspicion that the two publishers were in fact the "Montaigne poet" – they had been friends for many years, were both poets in their own languages. Both have consistently denied such an idea, pointing to the extremely different, some would say very conventional, minimalist poetry they write. (The French publisher had notoriously written a much publicized, lengthy attack on the prose poem as a "wrong turning" in French literature, urging a return to the use of the alexandrine.) By now there seems little chance of any fresh revelation. Personally I enjoy these prose poems or micro-essays whoever wrote them.

ROBERT BERECHIT
(1926 – 1947)

LOVE LETTERS FROM A
VANQUISHED CITY

TRANSLATOR'S NOTE

The following poems came to me in a curious way: an email from an unknown woman seeking permission to send some poems, mention of Jacques Rancourt in Paris who had given her my email address, her story – that she had been unable to find a French publisher for the original, that she thought perhaps the English-speaking world would be more appreciative of these poems, written by a great-uncle of hers, lost (it was thought forever), then found, then ignored for a generation, and now the question had devolved to her: what to do with them. Despite misgivings I clicked on the attachment marked "Berechit," fascinated by that Hebrew word "At the beginning of" with its dangling unattached possessive. Reading through this short manuscript I felt conscious of being in the presence of a kind of precarious, momentary defiance of the void – so close had this work been to disappearance. Imagining a French editor faced with these poems already half a century old, I could almost hear someone in an office saying: "But this has all been done before – French poetry has moved on." But does literature, does poetry have to follow some pre-ordained path? Circling back, why is that wrong? Aren't we always the contemporaries of our own ghosts?

In the second email, along with the attachment, I read Annette De Crécy's story of her great uncle, Robert – his childhood in Lyon, how he was placed in the boarding school Blaise Pascal in Clermont-Ferrand to keep him safe during the war, a school where the children of French Jews, Resistance figures and dignitaries of the Vichy Regime all coexisted in an uneasy, unstated suppression of what their fathers might do or who they might be. (Claude Lanzmann was at the same school, though Robert, a congenital loner, was never very close to him.) Robert's father, with whom he quarrelled violently, was, as far as Robert and others knew at the time, a collaborator with the Vichy regime. In fact he had been playing a double game, trying to save lives by arranging false documents and exit permits for several Jewish families. Tipped off that the Gestapo had discovered his double dealing he suicided in late 1943. Meanwhile, shortly after his sixteenth birthday in June of that year, Robert had run away to join the Maquis in the Haute Loire region, going by the adopted name of Robert Berechit. When the war ended he continued with that name.

It was well known at school that Robert wrote poems but no one had seen them. They were in small notebooks he kept with him during his travels. In September 1942 he began the notebook marked *Au Temps des géants qui arrivent*, a notebook he continued to work on throughout the war and in the remaining years of his short life. The last entry is dated May 27, 1947, his twenty-first birthday. On that day he set off from Saint Étienne, hiking in a southwest direction with plans to travel in a roundabout manner to reach Avignon in three weeks time. On the late afternoon of May 30 he was overtaken by a wild storm. While walking along a ridgeline he was struck by lightning but survived seemingly unhurt. Three days later, in a village well into the mountains, he stepped out of a grocery store, looked up into the blazing midday sun and collapsed. Hours later, en route to a hospital, he died.

Surprisingly, there were very few papers and no notebook on him when he died. Five years later his niece made a pilgrimage to the area, retracing his last steps. Eventually she found the notebook placed loosely under some stones in a barn outside the village where he collapsed. She was expecting a diary, revelations of his time in the Resistance, but instead found poems that meant little to her. She decided to show them to a friend, a student of poetry more interested in the latest minimalism, anti-poetry or the more transparent style of Philippe Jaccottet. Her friend told the niece Robert's poems were scraps of marginal competence, a schoolboy's writings. And so the notebook with its poems remained buried in a desk drawer in a modest apartment in Clermont-Ferrand. Fifty years later, on the death of Berechit's niece, the thin notebook was left to her daughter. Only in January 2011 did Annette De Crécy read the poems closely, then pause, read them again and decide they should be published.

It is a condensed re-constructed version of a selection of these poems I present here in English translation, settling on the title (a phrase used in one of his notes) "Love Letters from a Vanquished City."

LOVE LETTERS FROM A VANQUISHED CITY

1.

From my night camel
I gaze across at the battlements –
now swings and slides for the Kommandant's
prolific children.
In the supreme innocence of evil
life frolics
juggling the skulls of the dead.

In the city centre
between drab department stores and victory flags
a gallows and a small clean
abattoir for ritual murder.
Maniacally magniloquent
a tree speaks the language of stone
while the wind whirls
across night's spine
across exploding stars.

2.

If your face is there
in the glass cubes of my door
the greens and reds and blues

of my arcane rainbow door
through which a forest has entered

If your face is there
imprinted from a lifetime a century ago
in the glass cubes that read "spring"
If, though nowhere else,
you live in those glass cubes

a whirlwind is coming towards me
from the other world
even though, they say, the monsters are vanquished
the whirlwind has me in its sights

and you in the glass
who knew how to sidestep all whirlwinds
your waiting for a moment once
before the door of risk and loss

a face held in the blue green red
cubes of glass
glittering fresh promise of the place where daylight turns
forever no one's

3.

A first drop of blood
pools from the eye
onto the white tablecloth of midnight.

The acrobat sees his life
trembling in that drop.

In the darkness outside the tavern's light
an owl has set up court
to weigh and assess the drop of blood.
The owl is the acrobat's double
travelling on his invisible third shoulder.

Beyond them both midnight encloses us:
this intricate fine mist of snow,
small clustered perfections
forming and vanishing at birth.

4.

Once I was a fish
in the dream of the morning
Once I was mimosa in flower
stretched above the river's wild
dash to oblivion
In the simplest hour
heading homeward stripped of memories
with all my life behind me
pure openness

Once I was the face of the beloved
the sun come back to life in her green eyes
Once I was the lover

in the long night that leads over seven bridges
across and into and far from
the trembling city of light
Once all the birds of the world gathered in silence
round the nakedness
of our nest in the apple tree
Once there was nothing
but holding you

5.

To make my way through dawn
towards you towards myself
to weave through forest beyond the city
to alight in a town beyond the forest
grey chipped stone that lines the railway tracks
to be free
to assume a different name
to be someone else I don't recognise

in a bar
music is tapping
an old man guards
his thimble of cognac while outside
a young man breathes his jugful
of heady daylight
all around me the river is alive
every part of it
someone's eyes

burrow deeper into myopia
while triangles of light
pool in empty glasses lined up on a bar

Dawn:
on railway sleepers in a narrow cutting
the round bolts glow
like blue buddhas

6.

The city of the old world has set sail –
its china cup floating out beyond the waves,
crammed with miniature cathedrals, battlements,
a bell tower.
On the shore where I watch it pass
I slip my talisman under my shirt –
some lucky coins, a sprig of herbs
and the old battered handkerchief
bearing your initials.
With its single diminutive star
a tiny cup carries my voice
into the maelstrom.

ANTONIETA VILLANUEVA
(1907 – 1982)

ANTONIETA VILLANUEVA: AN INTRODUCTION

I first came across the name of Antonieta Villanueva in a monograph published by the University of Turin on the life and work of Federico Silva, French poet and essayist, whom the reader will have met earlier in these pages. They lived together for close to twenty years. Silva in his final Madrid years is described as being "both partner and carer" for Antonieta who had lost both her legs "in an accident" and was "confined to a wheelchair." From 1959 to Silva's death they lived together in a small apartment off Fuencarral, a short walk from Puerta del Sol and Cibeles. The monograph also mentioned that the Cuban-born Antonieta had written a well-received and briefly very popular three volume autobiography, part prose, part poetry, with the intriguing title *No voy a escribir mis memorias* ("I am not going to write my memoirs") (Vol I, Madrid, 1957, Vol II, Barcelona, 1965, Vol III, Madrid, 1969).

By 2010 when I first discovered her name all volumes were out of print and apparently unobtainable. Eventually I was able to track down second-hand copies of Volumes I and II. I am not a native speaker of Spanish and for me it requires several hours of focussed work to translate a page of poetry or complex prose, so there was no question of my attempting to translate the whole or even an extended portion of Antonieta's non-memoir memoirs. Nevertheless, as I became increasingly absorbed by her writing and since the work was already in the form of numerous discrete fragments,[5] I decided to prepare a short sample.

What particularly drew me to her work, besides the flair in her style and a certain haunted quality, was the series of coincidences between our lives. Both of us contracted polio in early childhood – Antonieta just after her third birthday, myself just before. Both of us seem quite distant from the Hollywood image of the "battler" child "defeating" a life-threatening disease to emerge whole and triumphant. Neither in Antonieta's account nor in my own life does it make sense to talk of personal effort or bravery triumphing over illness. There was, of course, all the work of parents and doctors, but physiological recovery, in so far as there is ever recovery, was essentially the work of invisible biological agents over which one has no more control than over any other virus or microbe that enters the body. And hospitalisations continued right though childhood and into adolescence, each time adding to the distance between oneself and other children. For both of us, polio made us who we were and it was no more possible to step aside from this than to trade in one's body or one's mind for a different one. What especially gripped me in Antonieta's story is that she is struck down not once but twice. After the childhood polio she invented herself as a young violin star, and then in mid-life, after a catastrophic accident, she made herself into a writer.

But there was something even more powerful that drew me to her. This is precisely the area in which her life is so

---

5 On the form of her Memoirs Antonieta wrote in the Preface: "When I thought of writing a portrait of myself I had before me a very definite model of how this could be done. From *Impresionas intimas* written when he was twenty six to the masterpiece of his seventies, *Musica callada*, Federico Mompou, working solely with miniatures, constructed a vast, inwardly consistent, image of his sensations, his world. The accumulation of discontinuous moments heard with the utmost precision is enough to say it all."

different from mine. It is not merely the Cuban background or her life as a concert violinist in the late 1920's and 30's. It is not something I feel able to talk about very much. Forces larger than her seem to work their way through her. She seems possessed. It is this suspicion which hovers over the edges of her book. Even when she was alive, she was haunted by others.

EXCERPTS FROM *NO VOY A ESCRIBIR MIS MEMORIAS/ I AM NOT GOING TO WRITE MY MEMOIRS*

Lifted up and gazing down, I fly, I fly over Havana. I am nine years old and I am three years old and twelve. My frame has gone, my sticks have gone as I have no need to walk. I see the Central Railway Station newly built and shining with flags and the magnificent department store on Florida. I see the gardens, the river, the flight of birds towards the city centre at sunset. I have slipped through the upstairs window opposite my bed and I breathe the air that at first almost burns my throat. Then, without thinking, I drink it and drink it. I become part of it, it becomes part of me. For this one hour I hold my life entire. And I weep from the perfection of it, the happiness of it, till, stricken by a sudden guilt, I go back to take my shape of a young girl lying encased in iron on a bed on the fifth floor of the Infectious Diseases Hospital and, seeing my parents enter the ward with such anxious faces, so that everything may happen, I resume my life.

* * *

It is the interminable hot summer of the year when I turn twelve. It is five weeks since I have come out of hospital, nine weeks after the last of the four operations to give me control over my legs, so I can walk. On a mission to cheer me up, my grandmother takes me to the theatre to see a visiting musical company from Madrid. It is, even then, a very old-fashioned zarzuela, stylised and wondrously over-costumed, perhaps my supposed initiation into young womanhood. I remember the small box of sweets my grandmother bought during the second interval and how one stuck to the roof of my mouth all through the complex denouement I no longer remember. I do not know why the theatre terrified me so much – the violent red of the heavy curtains, the dark sweltering heat of the salon, the distant fans whirring on the ceiling like calibrated knives. I remember feeling so out of place as if a theatre was meant entirely for some other class of people, some other race, while I sat there a young girl in an audience composed entirely of adults.

And into this memory suddenly rushes another memory, the heavy cream of make-up applied to my seventeen-year-old face, the white foundation, the smell of it, and my mother carefully applying strokes of red to my lips, that evening of the reception at the French Embassy, the announcement of my scholarship to the Paris Conservatoire, studies in violin and composition, to launch myself out into the world as some young Cuban Sarasate. Of that night I recall, most of all, my terror of make-up as if a wall were being clamped down over me, a painted frame to encase my skull and my eyes, and once inside I could no longer soar, could no longer speak with my own voice, only some stranger's words suddenly there echoing inside my throat.

*   *   *

At the threshold of the door
the black and white wasp they call "The Chooser."

Midday is the hour
pencilled in on his calling card
but he is patient, politely reticent,
a calmly non-insistent houseguest.
He eyes all that is inside,
especially the cool rim of the glass
foaming with ice and juice, summer scents
of quiet green fruits pierced open.
He injects his lance of poison, then affably,
intractably flies away
to other doors and other stories –
but always he is "The Chooser."

* * *

There is a tramcar that goes above the world and a narrow valley that plunges underneath it. Leaving from the beach, from the seaside park with its Ferris wheel, its miniature toy ponies trapped inside the garish colours of the merry-go-round, the little tramcar climbs above the sea perched on a perilous shoulder of red rock. Birds peck at its wires. Rivers go under us. The roar of their passage, the dizzying plunge of their waterfalls, grip us at random moments. One day early in life, just arrived in the city of culture, the famed world capital, I sit quietly huddled into myself on a bench in a park and sense the history of the planet moving by underneath me with its lazy suns and misguided moons, its withering seasons of universal shedding. Not often but every so often, all through my life, I have sat still enough to hear it. Almost, maybe once or twice, have my eyes become sharp enough to see it.

*　*　*

The lights are dazzling that evening in Budapest, the night of
the fall. I am on stage, leaning perhaps more than I should into
my violin. It is a partita by Bach and I have reached a moment
of absorption in the ambivalent pain-tenderness crescendo
that spins out from my hand, my arm, my thin frame, as I lean
into the sound-box of my violin, this wired coffin-space of the
earth's melodies, and at once I sense a crack as my calliper gives
way underneath me, buckles underneath, and I crash backwards
and sideways, my head bashing the hardwood floor, the broken
bone from above my knee splintering the skin. And as people
from backstage move to assist me I feel a great inward calm:
the music inside me stilled, the red curtains of the theatre, the
candelabra on the ceiling spinning, and softly I touch the back
of my head where blood is oozing and, as the seconds go by, I
feel more and more certain that I am not dead, am not about
to die, but that my career in the concert hall, my life as I know
it, is over. And I feel in the deepest sense untroubled, almost
relieved, like someone stepping into a quiet knowledge long
prepared inside them. I let the violin rest on the floor at some
distance from my arms as if the music had gone as far as it was
meant to go.

The operation in Budapest is well-intentioned but a mess.
They try to redo it in Paris but, with the thin bones of my right
leg, it doesn't take. When an infection sets in they amputate.
My husband of five years does not know this woman who
is always in pain, withdraws, seems to shut out the world of
music, is no longer interested in conversation, old friends,
lovemaking, feeling only a bitter angry disgust for her own

body. At thirty-three I am divorced and suddenly without an occupation. One afternoon in a café near my ground floor apartment in rue Solferino I take out a clear notebook and begin to write.

* * *

I am haunted by the others, those children and young women who lay in beds beside me in the various hospitals of my life but who did not live. The children swept away by fever, by deliriums of pain who did not come back. And when I left those places (for good I thought) at age thirteen, there is within me the pure pitch of their scream down the corridors of four a.m. Music where it stops us carries something of that scream, but moderated, articulated, reshaped into a dialogue of tension and relaxing, of soaring and giving way, coming to the edge of the precipice then drawing back. And what lies the other side of the scream?

Even now the best I have ever found to say is that the other side of the scream is magic, the silent inexplicable unfolding of magic. At age eighteen I am for the first time in my life standing in Paris, my hands open catching snow as it falls – a child of the tropics, I sense its miracle falling within me. And later I remember Ricardo Viñes playing for me the first of Federico's *Cançons i Danses*, the immense trust in space held in those opening bars, the shining back of the universe. I remember thinking if only I could write music – not just play it, interpret it, but write it. Invent a wholly new way of being in the world.

* * *

The languid hour.
In the tank in the living room
the wide-eyed goby jams a single eye against the glass –
a poking finger that scrubs and scrubs its
fixed dark corner of the afternoon.
Underneath, sheathed in the grey detritus
of a failed migration, a stone goes on
emitting bubbles.
The green waterlily is shedding
a ghost arm in spirals round the goby
as the afternoon, our lives, are stuck.
And then mother pulls out the stool, lifts
the mahogany lid on the still shining piano, that once more
an obliquely altered wild glissando
should interrupt the silence of the living room's
contagious clocks.

* * *

In the two years after my fall I start to dream patterns, to see
shapes for works that are half verbal, half music but without
any clear tunes – interplays of presence and absence, word
and void, the phrases and gestures of others cracked open to
reveal an identity between sound and mask, I who no longer
make love begin to image a lovemaking of voices and silences,
of screaming and the space beyond the scream.

* * *

A cold wind comes to me over the escarpment. Lanterns have been left out in the little café above the beach. As the painkillers release their calm I start to write. A younger woman with a family of children officiates as drinks are served and long red and white criss-crossed baskets of bread are placed on the table. Small candles glow as the night begins to settle. My pen flows across the page as I write these memoirs.

*   *   *

Where does music go when it ceases to be channelled through you? My hands no longer want to touch violins or stroke the keyboard of a piano. There is a rhythm in speech, in words themselves I want to unleash. And, even more, there is a rhythm in the world itself as it circulates around me, but not specifically around me – around itself, around people, birds, trees, like the wind realigning the leaves on a path by the pond in the Jardin du Luxembourg or the silhouettes of people seen from a distance gliding or bumping down the stairwell into the metro near Les Halles, or the other day the random faces of young men leaning over drinks in a bar opposite the railway station to the south, the brightly lit Palace of Departures, and the tiredness of a waiter wiping grease from the surface of a table. And I seek out other rhythms, like the clipped falsity of a speech that, beneath its bravura, hides a repressed childhood of endured persecutions, or at this very moment a tree in the south bursting into the ragged red blossoms of its lost orient. And I remember how we move unaware through the slow ballet of plants crossing and recrossing the earth.

I do not want to write my memoirs. I want the music that
died with my fall to find its other passage to me.

*   *   *

The butterflies that guard the portals of the underworld
hover just outside my window this morning. I know them
from the solemn tilt of their heads, the insistent beating of
wings. In the uncertain grey of dawn they guide me down the
street towards an iron grate that holds pure darkness in place.
And, as I peer down into the darkness, my eyes suddenly
wake to see the two butterflies once more at the window of
my bedroom – to which they have led me back. The moss-
covered canal banks of Havana are rocking to the waters of
Lethe. There is a barcarolle by Liszt played by my mother
floating up from the living room. My brother's kite is tilting
at the skyline. And, for me, the two white butterflies have
brought me home. In the cradle of mosquito netting, prickly
with the heat and damp, I awake, a larva-princess, blighted
and blessed.

*   *   *

In a bar in Madrid
the sky has crumbled like dust in my hands,
the Estremadura highway opens, to north and east,
the cold blooms of its desert.
In a bar in Madrid they whisper:
the lady in the wheelchair is on drugs,
the lady in the wheelchair is flying high above the sky.

In a bar in Madrid
the angels of winter are weeping at the door,
the ice is setting up its carnival lightshow all along
the cracked stone sidewalk.
In a bar in Madrid they whisper:
the lady in the wheelchair is smiling as she writes,
it must be a letter to home, a letter to family,
but what is she doing here
in the rain and the cold?

* * *

I peer up from under the beams of wood that form the veranda – from here, sky and the voices of adults blend and interchange, laughter, glasses clinking, the pouring of drinks, a phonograph scraping its way across a soprano's wavering voice. No one knows I am here. Dragging myself and crawling on all fours, I have found a way through the hidden passages of the house, the spaces behind walls, under floors to this cavernous, prodigious dead end. If I fear dark narrow spaces why do they also draw me, why am I compelled to go down into them? The fearful darkness with its small clay mountains, its broken ridges of cement and its soft hidden ant nests. As if I might come out under a waterfall and enter the valley of Shangri La. The world below the world feels like the true place that claims me. Until at age seven I discover violins and my life changes.

* * *

(In the hospital, late summer)

Like a boat tapping its great dull
wooden bell through fog
all night this sound

To float in starlight over the grey
cities of the world:
husks of an infant planet cover my eyes

To stand in a sea
while the sea stood in me:
isolate, impenetrable, dissolved

The black boat stumbles:
a corridor of ice on fire,
at last the rain.

* * *

One day the puppet-master arrives with his long stilts and
sky-blue hat. He sets up his display for us children in a
neighbouring garden. My mother insists I leave off my violin
practice for the afternoon to be with the other children.
Reluctantly with my older brother and younger sister, the
three of us set off along the back lane linking the gardens of
the houses. I want to stay outside of the group, but my older
brother, following my mother's instructions, insists I go with
the two of them into the neighbour's yard.

I have just taken my seat in the front row when I see it. The puppet of the wife in the play, Donna Rosa, has the same glass eyes as the witch that visits me at night. I sit frozen through the performance, determined no one should notice my fear, and even more determined only the puppet and myself should share this secret.

* * *

Mother and father are both out of the house when the surveyor appears at our door. He is carrying his instruments of air-spun gold and clearly the sky has rubbed off on him. He stands there mopping a brow that I know doesn't glisten with sweat but with the rain that only falls inside clouds. When I see him I tell him to wait there and go back to prepare a large glass brimming with ice and orange juice and soda. As I return with the drink I see that he casts no shadow. He moves from place to place, he tells me, measuring the contours of the earth. If I was not a violinist, I tell him, I would be a surveyor. And are you really a violinist, he asks me, his eyes taking in this girl of ten who totters on her callipers and thick black boots as she walks. I step inside and bring back my instrument which is chestnut brown and smells of the wild forests from which it was made. Not too sure of what he might like, I adjust the felt in the curve of my neck, position the violin exactly, then, careful to keep the pacing slow but varied, play the meditation from Thaïs. When he asks for a second piece I play a fast movement from Vivaldi. When he asks for more I smile and say that is enough. Then I ask him to show me how he measures the earth and, with calibrations of his tripod and notches and his small book of tables, he measures the shadow of our house first, and then my shadow.

He is the surveyor of roads and fields and harbours and all passageways between. From his table of calculations he recites the true distances and times. As he bids me farewell I see a small fragment of the sky has lodged in a corner of his face.

*   *   *

Thirteen slaves out of Africa hung themselves from the trees on my great-great-uncle's farm. He forbade their women to cover the men's faces in rags soaked in blood – trying to stop the repetitive pattern of mass suicides. The women believed that if those who suicided had their eyes covered in the blood-laced underwear of their women they would return to Africa, would find peace and plenty and freedom there again. And so the thirteen slaves became thirteen enormous birds with jet-black feathers, with claws made from the tiny eyes of the unborn, and they drift above the skies of my family's houses, wherever we place our houses, whatever names we give ourselves to protect us.

My grandfather was enraged when birds attacked the rows of banana palms he had planted. He took a gun and chased them off. They returned to attack the soft wooden frame of the shelter where his daughter was sleeping with girlfriends after a young person's party. The birds lashed the soft wooden walls with their beaks and, when the girls' screams chased them off, one of the damaged walls collapsed, and a heavy beam from the roof fell and killed Estella, my grandfather's youngest daughter.

When I was not yet ten days old my mother saw a great jackdaw, but much larger than a jackdaw, perched at the door looking in. She chased it off but she knew that I too was marked.

* * *

And the sounds that come towards us from the world beyond the world.

I am brought home from hospital and my father carries me around the large patio of the new house – and there, at the centre of this sun-filled greenery, a wide rectangular pond where fish of all colours, gold, orange, turquoise, vermillion, iridescent blue with crimson-and-grey markings, dart between the clustered stems of lilies. And gently, very gently, my father lowers me down to a smooth cool space on the bank. Far from the hot May afternoon that rages outside our house, I trail my hands in the water and watch the fish swim around my fingers.

To me the garden is voracious, compulsive. In the months after the hospital I begin eating dirt, its pure metallic grit sharp against my teeth. Later I am cured by a strange concoction of apples my grandmother prepares with fennel, hollyhock, cardamom, cinnamon and star anise.

The night visitors that terrified or comforted me in the hospital continue to surround my bed. In my room on the upper floor, my head resting on pillows under the window, when everyone else in the house is asleep, in the long hours between midnight and dawn, they come. The witch who leaves me her book of vanishing recipes, the bird-mother whose face alone brings terror or strength. The fragrant spirits of miscarried babies, bearing their traces of lavender and orange-blossom, trying to find their way back from the other world.

Of all this is the invisible music composed.

Of course there are also the days and the weeks, the excursions by car to the countryside, visits to cousins, private lessons, then a few years at a local school. But these things seem external to me, indifferent, barely touching me. And at seven, suddenly, unexpectedly, violins.

* * *

Under an enormous fig tree the day has gathered, heavy as a fig. My sister and I see our white dresses stretched out at the mercy of the figs. In all the sky, in all the orchard, heat blazes. Only, under the fig tree's shadow, the dark heady cool of the earth. Secretly, I reach down with one hand to fill my mouth with dirt, the dark cool taste of it, the fragrance of a spring that edges its way far down, unstoppable sister tributary of Lethe.

* * *

I am put to bed early as usual the night my father invites Joaquín Alameda, the virtuoso from Barcelona, to dinner. I am fascinated by the violin case he has brought and, once he starts playing after dinner, leave my room and sit listening on the stairs. When my mother notices me she beckons me over and I watch close up, enraptured. Joaquín shows me how to hold the bow and the violin. Within minutes I am able to reproduce, at first slightly mechanically, but soon fluently, confidently, the tune he has played. I stay up late that night and all of us talk, all of us make music, Joaquín and sometimes myself on the violin, my mother on her piano, and for songs and arias my father joins in as tenor. My mother immediately understands my passion and father soon acquiesces. Within a week I have begun lessons and hold in my hands a small violin, a gift from Joaquín.

Worried about the obvious pain I feel when standing still and the risk of damaging my already twisted spine, mother consults a designer of carriages and chairs who, following European models, has begun his own shaping of custom-built callipers. For me he devises a kind of metal chair that lets me rest my tail bone, keeping my lower back in a good posture, as I half stand, half sit. It is this frame, or a version of it, I use for my practising and, only gradually, go back to standing independently as I play, first for only five minutes, later for longer periods. After the last of my operations at age thirteen the improved strength in my left leg allows me to stand unaided for much longer. (My right leg, with its withered muscles, would always need a calliper.) By seventeen I develop the pattern of using the sitting frame for my practice hours while performing in public with no need of external support. When I reach Europe at age nineteen it is no longer my legs but the strength in my arms and upper body everyone notices. Standing tall and thin in the spotlight, the violin clasped at ready between hand and chin, facing the black space of the audience, I feel myself a mermaid carved into the prow of a ship, erect and fearless, slicing my way through the cold, turbulent waves of the world.

* * *

It is almost night when the owl visits.
And the dress I had hung out to dry
mirrors the grey face of the owl.
He stands on the railing just beyond the clothes-rack.
I close my eyes and see the earth
waiting to stop.

Puffed up with the rough certitude of what he brings,
his face peers into me, lays me bare.
A child who sits for hours
eye-to-eye with lizards, an elm, the sky,
I will not avert my gaze,
strong in the quiet knowledge
we are partners.

Here in the opening present
the owl that offers death
in a garden wide as the sun.

* * *

On my forty-ninth birthday I dream the descent into a deep
valley high in the mountains and find my grandmother is
there – then briefly Paulo, then Federico who I begin kissing
passionately, only it is a twenty-five-year-old Federico and
I am barely twenty-two. We are lovers, or about to become
lovers, when a small flotilla of black clouds pass over, heading
for Africa. In the dream I am whole and there is a thread of

music passing out of my right hand where Federico has cut a slit with a small knife he has been using to peel an apple.

And suddenly I wonder why I am not dead – of all those in this vast upland region of death, why am I still breathing? Why do I think it my right to kiss Federico when everyone in my family, everyone I know, is dead? There are vast grey eagles in this dream and they carry spirits from Cienfuegos high in a broad sweep towards the centre of Havana and, as they fly, they become blackbirds and, in the trees of the Parque Central, they fold their wings around the spirits of the dead who at last know what it is to sleep.

Elsewhere in my dream rises the many storied apartment block where I stayed in Madrid. From my wheelchair I will have to fly to the third floor – in a moment I do it – only to be told the third floor is closed now and I must relocate to the basement. Inside the basement there is a Balinese entrance plaque on the wall. When I press my forehead against it, I see a panel in the wall open to reveal a slab of rough concrete on which a packet of clove cigarettes has been placed. In my dream I realise my father and mother are in there, sitting quietly at the long table of my childhood, blocked by this wall where sound ends.

* * *

The violin tutor's house. Mid afternoon. The seeds of the cherries my mother packed for me to bring as merienda grow like a mound of skulls in the patio of Señora Valenzuela's house. Under the caoba tree with its shade I sit devouring cherries. Resting from the violin and the frame, I stretch my limbs. All at once, without knowing what I am doing, I have made an altar of skulls, this counterpoint to the soaring interplay of violins.

* * *

In the display case of the cabinet in our house in Vedado: miniature glass bears from Russia filled with Kümmel, a tiny bottle of green Chartreuse, elephants and a small pagoda of ivory, a flute player, a crafted boat that has just pulled in at the far reaches of the Western ocean. My father's oddments mingled with my grandmother's bric-à-brac from India, from her first marriage to a British officer, then after his death a holiday in the Canaries, a second marriage with three children – the first my father – and there were also the small watercolours she painted in India and others from Matanzas and the house in Cienfuegos, the vivid blue, gold and crimson splashes of parrots, jays, macaws.

All around me, in the background of my life, the unrealised, unrealisable ambitions of women to create something other than children or a home, the summons to something else.

* * *

Visits to downtown in my father's landraulet: the Parque Central with a short walk to the bookshop on Obispo, the cafés with their glass cases of cakes with chocolate and citron and almond paste, or browsing shops with my mother while my father went to the Gallego club. In the hot April wind the walk to the Plaza de Armas and the sea beyond.

There are three of them sitting in a row in the doctor's waiting room; under the whirring fan they lean at different angles on unstable chairs, hair grey and wispy as if attached to the head by a glue that is steadily melting, skin mottled by the Cuban sun, eyes dimly adrift in the 11 a.m. torpor; one with a thin gold-plated walking stick that tilts down towards the earth's centre. The right hand of the one in the centre cradles her left hand, passing under the wrist. The cords of her shopping bag are entwined around her lower arm (its long leather strap) and an unfolded tissue covers half her face. Three elderly Chinese women, and at once I feel myself Chinese, their sadness seeping in behind my eyes, and the doctor, an elderly Chinese man, whom my mother is taking me to see at age twelve, following a strange sudden wasting of the soul. This black cloud where I lose all interest in eating, turn aside from others, gaze elsewhere, gripped by fears I cannot name. This settling into night. For a moment I close my eyes to let myself be invaded by blindness.

In his room the doctor inserts acupuncture needles in spots on my wrists and below my ears. He speaks softly, something I understand completely but cannot remember, then taps my forehead with a wand. My life that was stuck moves forward again.

* * *

The saurian cat with his unsleeping eyes, immobile in the garden, grown plumper and plumper; the garden divided between the cat and the lizard, its twin deities, not just any lizard but a puffy frill-necked monarch, a chipojo, his long green neck reaching upward, hovering there with all the condescension of his slow ancestors, then all at once lightning-fast and brutal with tarantulas. I remember the time my mother's second-cousin, newly arrived from Galicia, screamed in horror when the lizard entered the house – this young woman newly come from the wettest spot in all Spain, a place where the weather could always be described with one word 'rain', entering the kaleidoscopic torrid zone of the island.

And in our garden, glittering with bougainvillea, heavy with sapodillas, mangoes, guava and the fruit we call anón, fragrant with jasmine, orange blossoms and frangipani, bountiful and confined, the cat and the lizard measured out their divided realm.

* * *

Already so far from the shoreline, my ten-year-old body rises and falls. A great silence descends layer by layer underneath me through vast currents of blue. Arms wide, legs resting open, I drift into fresh angles of the sun. Waves rise and fall. The sea spins slowly. I turn my face into the ripples of the earth's tilt, while, far under me, the white shadow of a manatee passes. Green foliage wavers and spins in its wake, a fragrance of earth's beginning. I can feel my body gently held firm in this spinning place, the wheel's centre.

* * *

There was a creek I was following one afternoon and a black umbrella bobbed mysteriously a little way before me – I could only see the top of it between the ferns and palms. The creek led to the sea, of course – that was where all creeks led, but sometimes they died in long meanders or faded into fields of tobacco, blossoming or abandoned. Or a few cows would stand suddenly on a road that shimmered with heat, munching the weeds that grew along the edges. I was always slow to reach destinations and would need to find places to stop and rest. It was a year when I was always sneaking out to do this, in brief bursts mapping the geography of the new house, understanding this strange sensation of walking.

*   *   *

Mother's small white vase that lingered on the edge of an enormous window, painted in gold stars. I never remember it filled with flowers – it seemed too magical in itself to permit anything else to be joined to it. I remember lying on a couch watching it, listening to my mother playing pieces by Chopin, Schubert and Brahms in the adjacent room. It must have been during those weeks after one of the operations, when I could not walk yet and drifted for days in and out of consciousness, lulled by small doses of ether to manage the pain. And the stars on the white vase shone for me – they promised distances, boats setting off across oceans and a world that, though smaller, was also wider, more opened out than the world of other children who walked so easily on two legs but did not understand about flying.

And I remember how we would cut out paper for Reyes, colour it gold and hang these golden messages on the front door, above the small carpet of grass and the glass of water for the camels. I remember how they glittered invitation and, for me, the knowledge that this was a place from which things started out.

> Plenty of stars, the small white vase spoke up.
> It liked the room we had chosen
> but most the wide window
> that gave onto the world.

* * *

And my memories, what are they after all? Which parts of them did I dream, which parts did I really see? Was it a great-great-uncle who called down a curse through his treatment of the bodies of dead slaves? Or was it my grandfather or his father who owned the slaves? And surely there was no underwear covered in blood? Surely it was as the books describe it, the clothes and belongings in a neat bundle, everything set in order at the foot of the tree, so the spirit could fly back to Africa?

* * *

I am playing Debussy's String Quartet. For a moment I close my eyes and immediately I am in a field of tall dandelions, clover and yellow flowering tobacco plants; above me wasps hover, my face is golden with sun. My playing continues, responding to, launching itself beyond the other players. My eyes open, then close again. I step in and out of a field of bright sharp scents, of restful, aching heat. While the wand I hold, the bow, glides slowly across the strings and my fingers race over the fingerboard, I leap back and forth between this brightly-lit stage in Milan and a field of flowering tobacco plants outside Cienfuegos, Cuba. They say nature does not make leaps, only sometimes it does.

ERNESTO RAY (1965 - 2016)

ERNESTO RAY: A BRIEF BIOGRAPHIC NOTE

Ernesto Ray was born in Fajardo, Puerto Rico, in April 1965. He moved with his parents to New York at age twelve. In high school he was a voracious reader in both Spanish and English – novels, poetry, short stories, biographies, plays – but increasingly he was drawn to music. At fifteen he became a regular visitor at the Nuyorican Poets Café, first performing there at age seventeen. Meanwhile with a few classmates he had developed his own band playing a mix of hip hop, reggae-jazz and I-am-furious-electro-ballad styles. He achieved fame early as a singer-songwriter who has been likened at times to a Puerto Rican Bob Dylan or Leonard Cohen. (Unlike many Nuyorican artists Ray wrote all his material in Spanish.) From the beginning he insisted "Everyone is just themselves," yet clearly he idolized Dylan and Cohen and, far more than any of his contemporaries, sought to emulate the imaginative range of their lyrics. But, equally, he played his lyrical narratives against a very different, far more aggressive musical "counter-voice," as he described it in his celebrated 1986 *Rolling Stone* Interview.

I do not intend to translate these lyrics as, stripped of their music, rhymes and elaborate word play, they feel impossible to do justice to in English. In any case, many are readily available on-line in passable translations, as well as in *The Definitive Nuyorican Almanac of 1997*. The year after the great Almanac came out Ernesto shocked his fans by renouncing music, New York and the Nuyorican scene, travelling to China and remaking himself as a humble teacher of English and student of Buddhism. "Giving it all away," he explained in an interview, "appeals to me far more than growing old trapped in repetition." This "rite of passage" as he called his thirty-third year saw him seek obscurity as single-mindedly as once he had sought fame.

On his return to New York in January 2003 he brought his new wife Pauline with him and the two of them focussed their life around the teaching and practice of meditation. He did do a few sell-out concerts and wrote a few new songs but many felt the magic had gone. It was a quiet time but also, undoubtedly for him, a time of inner growth and of a new-found contentment.

In 2012 everything changed. His beloved Pauline was diagnosed with cancer. His posthumously published *A Cloak for Pauline* is his first (and only) book of poems meant for reading on the page. During those years he also wrote three very lengthy songs, most notably "Ballad of the Drowned Lovers." I have reworked into parallel ballad form two of the thirty-three quatrains that make up this song. In *A Cloak for Pauline*, Ernesto, as he describes in his Preface (attached here as an Afterword), sought to shape poems that would work as spells. He never mentions Pauline's name in them and even writes what might seem to be a sequence of poems to other women. He does this, as he explained on several occasions, for reasons of superstition. To mention her name within any of the spells would seem to be placing her survival at risk. The most he will do is refer to her as "beloved." The sequence of women he writes poems to (or about), he once told prominent poet and critic Nancy Jones, are spirit beings, different aspects of one protective presence. In keeping with Ernesto's practice of reticence I do not wish to say here whether Pauline or Ernesto died first. For my own reasons I wish silence to surround these spells.

I have also included a few extracts from Ray's letter to Nancy Jones written shortly before his death. It's perhaps necessary to add that, four months before his third birthday, Ernesto Ray was hospitalised with a severe fever and nearly died in hospital. It was only his father who in effect kidnapped him from there, thus saving his life. This background helps explain one of the images in the first extract.

One final late addition: "Hammerblows" – a poem in a mixed ballad-rap style from the last year of Ray's life but omitted from *A Cloak for Pauline*. I include it after the letter at the end of this selection as perhaps Ernesto Ray's last work.

hand me my boots of silver
hand me my boots of tin
hand me my golden pedestal
when the rain sets in

so she brought in his boots of silver
she brought in his boots of tin
she brought in his golden pedestal
and let the sky come flooding in

(excerpt from Ernesto Ray "Ballad of the Drowned Lovers")

SELECTED POEMS *FROM A CLOAK FOR PAULINE*

OF SPELLS

A man, perhaps in his late fifties, is found lying in deep sleep in a gully near the San Juan-Caguas highway. He is unharmed apart from the few markings of life's normal blows: dental work, scars from one or two past operations, a slight disfigurement to three fingers of the left hand. There are letters in his pockets – one in the pocket of his shirt, one in each pocket of his trousers. His breathing is regular as of one relaxed into deep sleep, but neither the travellers who found him nor the medics who were soon summoned could wake him. Besides the letters there is a wallet with driver's licence and various cards. They can identify him. They soon know where he was born (Fajardo, 1954), where he lived, who his parents were. He had been a bus driver, living alone in a small apartment in San Juan after a divorce, the only son of a very ordinary family: mother a secretary, father a mechanic in a small car repair business, both parents now deceased.

The letters in his pockets are all on fine gold leaf paper, in languages unimaginable for a humble bus driver from Puerto Rico. One letter is in a dialect of Aramaic – it looks like the work of a scribe of 300 A.D. The second is in Sanskrit, perhaps (so experts say) drawn in ink on paper brought back from China around 200 B.C. The third is in Japanese from around the twelfth century.

One is a letter of recommendation for a driver of chariots living on an unspecified island in an archipelago renowned for its lush vegetation and extreme heat. It commends him to the notice of the higher ones. The second in Sanskrit describes an individual's past or future life as a tree. The third consists of incantations, a spell, a recipe, a promise to a beloved. As the man sleeps over the next five years the letters are interpreted, translated, recited. Their chanting fills the night air around the man. Their breath is the slow caress of hands over his body. Sound's weight accumulating, fine traces of shadow hands: a dust descending from the sky. Their breath slowly gathers into the one word, the imperative singular of the Sanskrit verb: Live.

After they undressed him at the hospital to monitor his vital functions someone noticed a strangeness in the texture of his shirt. Under a certain light you could read, fixed deep in its fabric, spirals of words from many languages, letters and ideograms like countless fingerprints weaving him a many-coloured skein of protection.

I had planned to transcribe these letters in their Spanish version here. I had planned to copy out the text of his shirt, to set these things down here as a spell to protect my beloved as she drifts in and out of the haze of medication. I had hoped to weave round her the chanted spells of the bus driver from Fajardo. Life does not always give us what we plan. Our room opens on a small garden and the chill coastal breeze sets a small web of pentatonic chimes reverberating. As if the East was trying to reach us, trying to set up the spells that heal even what the spiders of cancer have devoured.

Let these words stand in for the spells I cannot find.
Let the letters of the bus driver of Fajardo though I cannot
find them
stand in (the image of them) as
four paper screens unfolded
four spirit hands upholding
(stand in for) guardianship
of earth and air
the spell of all peoples
whispering its silken wall
woven (the sky's tent casting
its four shorelines of protection) round
one person,
my beloved.

DISCOVERED IN A ROCK POOL

A star-shaped object rising up
out of the water – five
wavering arms, five
spokes of a chariot wheel, five
curved cylinders, at their centre
a cluster of grey barnacles, small pearls, a silver light,

the water that drips from them
heavy with salt, oxidized
incrustations. A star tiara
from a drowned mermaid, the wheel
of some vast chariot washed up.
And, as it breaks the surface, this sharp sudden

fragrance like plants left
too long in narrow vases, the water
like urine drained out of dried twigs.
The wheel is a ghost of a wheel.
The fiery chariot's return to
the kingdom of salt. And everything

shrinks and is less than a token
miniature apple, a walnut placed
as a skull-shaped offering on an
altar to placate the goddess of devouring.
Effigies stored in a rock pool.
This is surely someone's

childhood not mine. Such simple things
might be placation or destruction. Starfish
or a galaxy intact
as its detritus. Burnt out. Cooling off,
cooling off in a solution
of brine and midday sun.

– Whom do you seek?
The woman at the centre of the starfish-wheel asks me.
– I am after another life.

ARNICA ARTEMISIA

To arrive some November morning,
rain-washed banners wilting on the wide terrace.
The house eaten from the inside:
earth spilling from the lining of cupboards,
worms trapped inside water-drops
cascade from the ruptured web of pipes.

Arnica:
its spokes pounded like a wheel.
Eleven needles in the fabric of morning.
Wings of lepidoptera: wings of broken comfort
and a small star from the back of my eye
takes flight.
The migrating horde of dust mites
takes flight.
In the fuse box all the wiring spikes
like a flowchart of vital signs.
A family of possums enters
to offer cheer, to exchange bewilderment.
My head alone in a house alone
as a small mermaid crafted by the fisherfolk of Peru
floats dangling from a final rafter.
Light from the spiderwebs,
rainbows on the floor.

Arnica: star-bright
small jewel of light

my memory.
Arnica Artemisia
mugwort sagebrush
salve against malaria and the fever of not yet being born
star at the core of my hand
at the door of the ruined house
you signal a narrow bridge into myself
the rainbow is your younger sister.

IRIS

She was called Iris and, why I don't know, we were climbing in and out of an earth-pit winter home that was also a Seven Eleven somewhere in the provinces of China. A wealth of automatic dispenser machines hungered for our coins, holding – imprisoned behind glass – white mounds of dumplings, Styrofoam containers of glass-thin noodles, hunks of pork, quartered moon cakes with the egg of promise on display in the middle. Her name reminded me of the rainbow but also seemed to signify her hair which was golden and bunched into looping curls at the back, held in place by a long clamp of multicoloured plastic. I was intrigued by the distance in her eyes and the fretful way she seemed to chew over her words, while all the time waves of silver light flickered above her shoulders and face.

Beyond us both, the street twisted uphill towards the water tower, the pagoda, the region of teahouses and a university village that had a wide view across the rising tiers of the outer sea that flows unbounded, stretching as far as those lands we have no names for, so distant any visit would require a new birth. I have seen places where doors are opened, winter habitations dug into earth and opened by a flap that lets the sky be admitted or dismissed. I have seen a family hunkering down into a small space of cooking pans, many-sized bowls, mats and blankets for sleeping laid out at different levels, long pipes that are also heirlooms and runic messages. In the centre, controlling every gesture, a conical tower of embers.

The habitation – part store, part earth-dug igloo – was different from any place I have stayed in before, and Iris presided over it, hands on hips, a torrent of energy, my tutor and also a supervisory nurse briskly organising and thoughtfully consulting an anonymous assortment of those who have been intensely damaged physically. Their cloaks and pinned ward-gowns flapped gently, plastered as these items were over missing limbs or inner organs. In the background a range of further figures seemed to have fallen off the hillside and now be drifting into the lower reaches of the sky.

In Iris' hands, as she stopped to speak to me, were five matchsticks and a small pot of glue. Quiet and deft, I said to myself. I took them as emblems of my terror, of my faith.

If I knew her as Iris it was because she was (among her many other names) a bridge in the city to which I had been summoned: on one side of the canal, temples, pagodas, changing cubicles with masks and long robes left hanging from hooks for the summer festival; on the other side, illness, death, the procession of the haunted. And her face was made of conflicting colours, split like the lightning bolt in the centre, her gold hair in its bun parted at the centre, and like that she walked, with the utmost dignity and reassurance, between the living and the dead.

ELEUTHERIA

Water spirit of small bowls
beyond the bamboo curtain of my window
a black bowl harbouring green shoots I have no name for
maybe the small slick of water
on the surface
is enough for you
maybe the few early morning raindrops
are enough for you
an ornamental tree spreading fan-like branches
two small stone steps into a garden
with room only for a few
well-tended weeds (if everything non-native
is a weed) sun water
a few flourishes of stone
I would have liked an ocean a tidal inlet
a riverbed at least or clear creek
cut like childhood between suburban allotments
but where you glide is my renewal
telling me a cup will do
a line of silver in air
to swim and glide and curl up
within a water-drop
in the tracery of moisture at the end of a leaf
what this morning the birds harvest in the long
silence of the skies

ODILE NÉE VÉRONIQUE

That was the sickness of the grass the withering of catkins
their stems crushed for
moth-food the distillation
of early summers gone wrong

Odile née Véronique your name
legible still on broken rock as
a grave marker summons
the green spirit under its
white husk its canopy of
always repeated wedding
I think of you coming into your
resting place febrile among the flying ants
that one day will ferry you to
the birthing temple where water
bubbles up between the stones

you whose name crosses lineages crosses
worm and greenness odalisque
and neonate
daughter of church bells and the open road
a sign pointing me over hills
is it too much to ask that you
negotiate on my behalf with the
lord of the underworld in his green
violent tangle of lichen and roots

that he spare this distant mirroring of
yourself since all women are sisters of dust

and that the stormcloud of this summer be withdrawn
glance otherwise
tell him say it
Odile née Véronique
princess dressed in the cicada's livery where

the chambers of dawn glow green at first light

YU LING

a slight trembling of the air
                          at afternoon's end
or rounding a corner we think we see you
climbing beyond the tree-line
                          into some
night sky of an altered hemisphere

You sit facing us as we fall asleep
when our eyes no longer register the world
or sometimes perhaps we catch
your quietness there
among heavy urns in a room
where the dead sleep standing up

I cannot ask you anything
I am simply breathing with you

the sound of jade tapping jade
while underneath and all around

the waves coming in
                          more and more
                                    under the jetty

The magic of your hands lies on both of us
May it touch more deeply
                          fill more amply

From your forehead

                        and the curve of your eyes

a still space opening for us

                        invisibly with us

Yu Ling: jade princess

AUBADE

driving back into the city
neon through fog
the high wide bridge stranding us
above the floating mirage of buildings
and what we had thought were our lives

were those your words
nothing but a gamble
a long jaggle of notes descends
like the messages spoken by a lift
taking us forever down
intimate fishing
in this splutter of coughs
and buried faces
I'm getting tired
I don't blame him
the squeals of the trapped
something dying on the inside
half of you walked away long ago
take care guys, you take care
in love with what is always
about to start living
yes, we were trapped

MEDITATION

I had just closed my eyes in meditation
silence fell on the world
I saw it
there in the centre of my chest
in the space between
two almost touching hands
laid out in a long row
the fraction sign the sign for the square root of
a dense crowd of symbols
neatly lined up
the formula that spelt the length of my life
but more precisely
when this leg will go
when a tic will develop over the right eye
then the left
when the sex will die when speech will wander off
when this or that group of memories will leave
when the shoulders will stop lifting
when the hand will forget how to close

when everything will go back inside the heart
and the heart will slip away
to wherever the dust comes from

MY LOVER'S SHOES (THIS MORNING)

flip flops thongs jandals
sandal of many names and a single
plastic loop
orange they open
a platform of butterflies and spirals
fivefold petals brushed in white
sun's intense childhood radiance
on a winter floor

although this dark world grabs at you
you have stepped
onto the soles of an altered shining
that these simple swirls of colour may
spiral up your legs into your inmost
core of being

others have spoken of the "shoes of wandering"
for this morning, my lover, you have chosen
dazzling splotches of summer
bearing the grace of all you were,
of all you are

EXCERPTS FROM THE PREFACE TO ERNESTO RAY'S POSTHUMOUSLY PUBLISHED *A CLOAK FOR PAULINE*

Magic is not easy. Spells are not made casually, don't happen just because we want them to happen. They require precision, elaboration, training, inwardness and long silence. Poetry that can work as magic must be difficult poetry, must gather many things, must come out of solitude, must focus and weigh many words. A poem that can make trees bend towards us, or gather the audience of birds at a window, or cast a double rainbow over a house, or heal bones, will never happen if a poet is caught up in the tried and true, the familiar, the pleasing of others, the gathering of mass audiences. What pleases people immediately, what can be understood immediately, is incapable of casting the deep resonances that make magic happen. The language of a poem-spell needs to be more wrought than that. One-dimensional poetry, linear poetry that can be pounded out at a New York rap club, that thrills the youngsters or fits neatly into the thematic units of educators and academics, none of that can work any more. Not for me at least. Not for what I need now.

The poets who cast magic are many – a small minority but many: Lorca, Desnos, Rimbaud, Saint John of the Cross, Emily Dickinson, Hopkins, Paul Celan, Mandelstamm, Vallejo of course, always Vallejo – but not Neruda, not Paz, not Pacheco, Cardenal, Parra. Not any of the people who get set on courses to illustrate some kind of well-intentioned social history of our times. Poetry that is magic cuts through history.

When death folded its claws around the shape of my beloved I didn't want to write song lyrics anymore, I didn't want to be a darling of the Puerto Rican community anymore. I don't want sagas of my people. I don't want audiences drawing me back into well-worn stories of who we are, what we suffer. Identity bores me. Identity isn't magic. The poet magicians weren't hung up about the dividing lines between their people and other people. Death, evil, the abyss were far too close. They wanted spells, counter spells. This is what I am seeking. If I am to write anything it can't be diary entries for my lover's illness – I'm not her. It can't be some biography of how I lived with the knowledge of my lover's illness. I don't want a story. I want cures. I want to fashion magic objects made of words. I want to summon protective presences.

This is (also) (looking back at it now) what my three years in Asia taught me – my year in China, my months in India, Nepal, Thailand, in the monastery outside Kyoto. My beloved is too ill right now to weave her own spells. And (always) there may only be right now. I don't want to communicate with the merely visible. I'm no more after an audience than was Hopkins, Dickinson, Rimbaud. I don't want a familiar frame that people can hang things on. Forget I'm Puerto Rican. Forget I'm cutting edge. I don't want to be called any label – not even neo-baroque. I know when a force enters words. I know when a spell is being uttered and the walls of a house understand this.

Magic requires a thorough clearing of the self. The ego must go, the self must go. Rimbaud understood this.

Desnos and Vallejo understood this. The Chinese masters spent their entire lives perfecting this. The books of the Bible, as understood through Talmud and Zohar and a long collaborative questioning, carry this density. They carry spells, as do the sutras of Buddhism and phrases of the Tao Te Ching. But how can a poet at the start of the 21st Century reach that place? In my own case, how can I find my way there fast enough to write the spells that will weave magic for my beloved?

And I feel that, for all the poets I've read and can name, I start nowhere. Through my twenties I was cursed by my success. I never went deep enough. At thirty-three I left the New York–Puerto Rico scene, handed in my Nuyorican badge and travelled to Asia, worked there teaching English and Spanish, studied, meditated, fasted. In China, in Beijing, I met my beloved, the Australian teacher of languages, Pauline. We had two more years in Asia: wanderings, rainy-season retreats, Zen monasteries and ashrams. Then, back in New York, for eight years we lived our simple life of gigs here and there, more teaching, some practice (Zen, Vipassana, chanting the Vedas) and then, at first imperceptibly but soon all at once, a cascading rush, the great onslaught of pain, the scans, the biopsies, the MRIs. The late night dashes to Emergency Wards. The diagnosis, the timeline. And the web-like lines of chords around her, as if she had been transported to the underworld.

Where to start if I am to weave spells? Not with the old linear, one-dimensional poetry. Neither transparency nor wilful language games. I need new alignments. I need the ancestors behind, beyond ancestors, brought into play. Maybe

I'm really Jewish, maybe I'm really Chinese or Taino. And I call on the spirits of earth, air, fire, water. I come devoid of lineage yet with a tangle of stories that press against me, demanding their voice. I do not have a true name. I need to empty myself so a complex realignment can start. I wait on a barren shore, my palms open, my face tilted towards the chariot of Elijah, asking that somehow the words of power will come.

EXTRACTS FROM A LETTER WRITTEN BY ERNESTO RAY TO HIS FRIEND NANCY JONES SIX MONTHS BEFORE HIS DEATH.

. . . By night faces and images swirl in front of me – troops of lost children, they wander the corridors of that vast hospital that's still there under the great wintry lake of this city. Gargantuan carp swim across the tiny chamber where my first bed was. Before the lake. Before forgetting.

What I wrote comes back to haunt me:

> Like a shadow on water, the beautiful.
> Two shadows on water, love.
> They came with their mouths brimming "rescue."
> By dawn all that's left was blood.

. . . . . .

You know my first big hit "Street Kid":

> It's spelt on the cans you open.
> Its words keep appearing in the soup you've begun:
> Listen, Turgenev, stop flexing your muscles.
> The day is too old for this, your life too young.

To give the Latino street kid the name of a Russian novelist – not Juanito or José or something, anything, you'd expect. No street kid called himself Turgenev but suddenly they were all doing it. And I thought, So? Is this it? Is this what fame means? It's bullshit.

When I was in my early thirties I kept getting these dreams. I kept being woken up at night by José Martí and I'm not even Cuban. "Compadre," he'd say, "this is bullshit. You can't make a revolution with these crappy songs. And on this side I know. You're not Cohen or Dylan – and don't let them fool you into thinking it's the translators. It just doesn't hold a candle to them. The days of revolution are over – not here, not now, not New York. Give it over. Do something different." And Martí showed me a monastery between mountains and cypress trees, somewhere in East Asia. I didn't know it but it was the monastery outside Kyoto. He kept telling me my songs were worthless and I had to get away, travel far from it. The last time he ever appeared to me, a week before I really decided to go, I was awake, I swear, and I still saw him mumbling in the corner. With a sad look he turned back towards the infinite corridor of his own travels and with a shrug he just muttered, "The only revolution is yourself."

. . . . . .

Perhaps I have no identity. Perhaps I was born in China in the twelfth century. As I approach my own death, no longer slowly but hurtling towards it as in film footage of a train crash where over and over all the carriages sandwich together, fold into each other, I have no sense anymore of who I am, who I was. Everything prior to this moment evaporates, floats off, and my mind, my habit of weaving stories, keeps fabricating different roles I played, different names I had, works I wrote, women I loved, cities I lived in, journeys I made or failed to make. My long dead parents come back, their faces taking familiar form in different landscapes, speaking different languages, decked in strange costumes. My mother floats above a lake of water-lilies and in her altered voice I recognise a forgotten sister of Marcel Proust. Then suddenly she is standing next to a precipice and a wind-bent signpost: it's maybe 1700 and she's just stepped out of a carriage halted near an inn somewhere between Spain and Portugal. Soon she will enter a nunnery where, through long fasting and prayer, she will attempt to dissuade the demon who will reincarnate into General Franco from launching the Civil War.

Approaching death the self loosens its grip. The world's demonic history rushes at me, wanting to unpick me, to send my unravelled voices spiralling into the silence of God's hidden void. I want to say mother, father, lover, but everything rushes beyond that. I can make out a narrow path between rice fields. I balance on it, my arms outstretched, some spindly-legged black-white bird of prey about to take flight. What is it to come to consciousness in a body freighted with such strange incongruous weights? To imagine myself padding down the aisle of a shopping mall that is also a great medieval cathedral in the silver slippers of a young Chinese girl from some forgotten picture book? I feel my head spin with words that hobble me as I go the nowhere path across hills undulating like a single long last breath. My lover is the landscape, the road, the spiralling air, the white moment of vanishing.

HAMMERBLOWS

- Hay golpes en la vida, tan fuertes . . . Yo no sé! (César Vallejo)
  (There are blows in life, so hard . . . I don't know.)

In subway cars
on a path below high mountains
storm coming down
in the 10 a.m. sun moving step by step
along a row of chairs lined up on a sidewalk
in the name on an envelope
under a thick smear of jam
in the suicide of buttons in a drawer of waiting knives
There are blows

In what you know hear want can't say
fecund snowflake razors
there are blows

In the breeze that rises
when someone's gone
In airports and the chill eternal
failure to set out
In the rewiring of memories
so every landscape every half-arsed jerking of
an ill-timed word
floods all the avenues
rains like ripe tomatoes
on the most umbilical umbrellas
there are blows

Like the sleek geek who won't speak
rancid skies dripping death
like petrified vultures oozing lard
in the forecourts of the Four Winds Stock Exchange
or a banker on hard times sniffing glue that oozes
from a pothole of pock-marked
preferences to trade in the dark

Unarguably
there are blows
A tree to the knees
A quick slit to the left of the breath
A brief stab to the right trapezoid
and it flows
like rum of the Rialto
gone sodden gone
drenched fire
hung from heaven on a wire
like a dream going forward
or a tack stuck in a throat
that won't pass
there are blows

Under benches
in safe cubicles
in a scrambled letter left behind on a train
in paper cups soiled plates
a fridge crammed with wedges of stale bread
or a road that twists its cracked spine under rain
there are blows

and in the imperceptible
accumulation of seconds
as a roof snaps
as a day drifts into darkness

in the flip of a card
in solitaire
in conversations morsed by the time-bleep of machines
in the crisp voice flooding like treacle
over the floor of an office
or the practised spiel rehearsing
the trajectory of endings
in our endings

Set upon by minions gagged by gargoyles
on the roof, feet kicking
drained of air like a deflated owl
crowd-surfed down corridors
dressed by ghost-fingers in
some tight-fitting cloak of lost arms
in the steady breath of midnight stillness
or the scratch-scratchings of pain rocking
on a makeshift trestle by the window under stars
my love
in every moan replayed
there are blows

In the trickle of the chicken that's rotting
in the shoulder-bag of the boy of the third strap
of the last carriage that wavers above the

all blasted
their hands nailed to iron rafters
and yet the light is there

In the land of far away last night
where an old tart flicks her foxtail bathrobe in your face
in the pissoires of seventh heaven
where red pustules sprout from boys' flies
and a certain stench
clenches your nails on the zipper that won't budge
when you feel like a foetus growing old in a waterhole for
    ratsack
as the gaunt attorney
slips your fingerprints into the
state-owned deposition on the inventory
of purloined combs
that nails you there, right there
among tender ostriches
hanging by a thread

And there are blows
immaculate interceptions
disconnected calls to Mars
music that turns one last time at the threshold
turns back to gaze at us
once-only short-term spinners
left behind in the room for lost jars

like a wave going out
along the edge of the world

like some bleary-eyed bard of the doorway
who wears our face
and has no language

all the hammerblows it takes
to make a hammerklavier
the nails nailed into it
and when it soars
the still attentive fingers numbering death

and how
on the lowest edges of the heavenly choir
among the counsellors consolers
where the jackboots just now begin to reach
there are blows

How say it
beloved
now my face is
three swift kicks of death
on the night-patrol of nowhere
two hands round a thick jug gathering light
and yet and yet . . .

There are blows

ELENA NAVRONSKAYS BLANCO
(ADDITIONAL TRANSLATIONS)

EXCERPTS FROM *LOS MUERTOS* (BUENOS AIRES, 1996):
"CONVERSATIONS WITH GREAT-AUNT MYRIAM"

CONVERSATIONS WITH GREAT AUNT MYRIAM

PART ONE

We walked that day through the cemetery past the stone crypt
which some gravediggers had opened –
a crowbar had gashed the rock where it wedged a side-panel
   open –
and I saw the white clay under the brown soil,
and I thought, "No, you cannot rest here,
they can't place anything that was you here,"
and my throat gulped that something that was once part of you
should go down into the wounded white clay.

*　*　*

It was a time before time, a time outside time, and it would
always be there, always ready for me to slip into it. And I
wondered, if I turned a corner fast enough would I bump into
you? And I tried pacing myself so many different ways but it
never happened.

   I think you must be standing somewhere looking through
your small gold-clasped purse but the coins have all changed.
The faces on them are wrong and you remember suddenly
how that high-nosed face was from before the revolution but
you can't remember which revolution. And you think perhaps
you have been on this corner, counting coins, for five hundred
years now. And, all that while, the sun stays at your shoulder,
exactly the same.

You kept going out into the dark to look at the slope of wild trees because, you said, it needed you. It was the night of the steppes you carried with you everywhere. Here, on the slopes of the first foothills of the Andes, it whirled around you and your face glowed with its light, sister to the Arctic sun and the fierce wolves of the north.

And, when you came back inside, your eyes brought the weight of lost stars, the reverberation of vast snowfields that bind the earth, into our small farmhouse nestled in its postcard row of orchards, of fields for cows and other neat houses, each in their own order of makeshift gates and coiled garlands of smoke.

And I see you again among the kitchen clutter you would always touch with disdain as if it wasn't quite there.

When I go back to visit the old farmhouse and the new owners let me glimpse inside I keep thinking I'll see something of you, the hesitation of your hands resting on a doorknob, your face in a mirror, but nothing. Now you drift forever in your night and even the lizards under the stones by the doorway can't call you back.

* * *

Our farmhouse remains but, by now, the fields beyond are just the city's ragged edges: tottering apartment blocks going to ruin, an abandoned tyre factory, small squat houses where, before, an orange grove and grapevines had wandered off into what were, for me, interminable distances, all that vast inner space separated from me now by the bare breath of that single syllable "then."

*　*　*

One time I came to visit the old farmhouse, as I did every few years because of all the memories it held. This time the owners gave me a small box they had found buried among rusted farm tools in the back of a shed they were planning to demolish, out in part of the farm where my father used to grow wheat back in the years when grain prices were good. There was a pile of old notebooks in my father's hand – ledgers of accounts, bills, lists of crop yields and the prices paid for them. But also two 75 rpm records of the kind people were just starting to make in the nineteen twenties – one was of grandmother Ada singing a few popular arias, including a folksong in Yiddish that probably came from Odessa. The other was of her sister Myriam talking, her gentle voice sweeping slowly onward in that Russian-inflected Spanish I remembered as one of the many sounds of my childhood. I remembered then how my mother told me once that on their thirtieth birthday, at the invitation of a travelling salesman of novelty items, a friend of a friend of my grandfather, the twin sisters had made these recordings that were then lost during one of those recurring periods of turmoil when it became necessary to sell off one part or another of the farm.

Back in Buenos Aires I looked up a friend who had the right machine to play these old records and, as I listened again one evening in my friend's Floresta apartment, my great-aunt Myriam was there again, sitting before me, speaking.

PART TWO

If you are hearing this it is because I am speaking to you in Spanish though Spanish is not my language. I could have said these things in Russian though Russian is not my language - nor is German, nor even the Yiddish spoken by my maternal grandfather (my family was always marrying the wrong people, stepping outside rules, transgressing in the hope one day to invent ourselves). My language comes from wolves and from the wind, from butterflies and moles, from storks and swans, from the wind in the birch trees, from the turning moon. I will not speak for long. They have told me I have ten minutes. I will not speak much but I will say something.

* * *

I remember the servant Ana. A niece or distant relative of some kind from the old country. She was simply there one day, serving at table, folding clothes, gazing into distances from the front steps of the farmhouse. As she got older she got smaller till we had to hide her from the ravens and eagles of the mountains that came to peer into our windows. She started to look more and more like a butterfly – often in blue and pink, with green or golden ribbons, and her hair dyed flame-red because she was always so proud of her looks. And her ninety-year old cheeks still soft as in the morning of the world.

* * *

The elderly teacher said to me: "You walk among sparks of the great fire. That is why your feet feel so heavy and often hurt. Only be patient: where there is fire there is always a passageway down to the great lake under the earth."

I distrusted my elders: a wise instinct given to the young, but eventually I understood she only meant a certain kind of fire. And the heaviness in my feet made all movement difficult, even back then when I was a young child and the others in my class could fly so easily from room to room, from the swings at the bottom of the playground to the trough with the taps where we drank, from their homes with all kinds of food to the great hall where we all gathered one day for the first communion breakfast. I was both happy and unhappy to be strange.

One day the teacher spoke to me when no one was listening and said, "This fire is here too, where I'm placing it now. Your secret." And with those words a small spark of red burning lodged itself in my right palm where the life-line crosses the meridian of the god-planet Mercury. And not that many years later there was the accident. It was, oh, in the last year of primary school, a different school, and by then I'd lost all contact with my special teacher. I was running down a corridor, gripped by a sudden nausea, with a pen in my hand when I fell. The nib stabbed deep into my right hand, tore through the flesh, disgorging its stream of black ink into my veins. At the hospital all one night they talked (I could tell from the whisperings) of amputating my hand, but instead, when the specialist arrived, a lady doctor who looked very like my old teacher, she said: "Nonsense - it will only need a little memento, a nicely knitted scar, just here."

Then the years passed and one day, far away from everything, I woke among flames. And through them, far down under them, I saw the lake.

* * *

In the rickety small truck my parents borrowed from neighbours we are travelling through the forest across the vast spaces of night. Wind and black clouds curl around us. I am sitting next to my sister in the open tray at the back of the small truck. My sister lies there stretched out, her twisted body shivering now and then as she moans softly, continuously, from inside her world of pain. With one hand I am holding her hand, with the other I balance myself against the repeated jolts of the truck. Stars race by over us. The moon shifts steadily in its crossing. How many hours does this last? I close my eyes, count to a hundred slowly. My sister and I are still there unchanged under whirling trees, under the same stretch of sky. Forty, fifty years later I close and open my eyes. I am still in the back of the truck and my sister's eyes are half closed, trembling, round like glass marbles, like a scream.

* * *

Another teacher said, "When you read a group of words there are always at least three ways of reading them, since words always hold other words inside them. However, when after an hour's intense reading you close your eyes and inwardly see what you have read, a hundred, a thousand images will flood in. Such is the nature of true books, of true reading. It is why over and over the world wants to destroy books."

*　*　*

The clouds were not easy to read. Looking out of the window with rain falling through a sudden fracture of the sky, I called them "nymphéas" though the blossoming clouds were not really very much like waterlilies. Sometimes my grandmother would take me to the park to look at them. Their round sprawling green bodies naked under a layer of scum. Like bloated green sunbathers indecently reflected by some mirage of the sky. On the water floated wild ducks and, underneath, an eel with its enormous tooth that lashed out at visitors, especially any dogs or children who came too close. And in the park by the lake I was always afraid of falling in. Which nearly happened once. Only some presence I felt but no one there saw pulled me back. My strange perpetual guardians.

*　*　*

A trace is often left in the sky when a world has vanished. Not always golden or black – rarely towards the red end of the spectrum, as if the light that reaches us at such moments has had to cross, not so much distance, as a kind of inwardness. Silence-gatherers appear then, coming out of their houses with jars of all shapes and sizes to trap silence. In basements all over the city they hoard it in round cork-lined vats. It is used in the preparation of certain exquisite dishes. It deepens the texture of all foods, adding to their taste shadings of never-before-experienced mushrooms, of rowan berries and earth fungi. All food, they say, becomes something different when cooked with an infusion of that heavy silence. Just as, so our anchorites used to teach in the old country, the disappearance of remote worlds is what gives this life's sadness flavour.

* * *

I remember, oh some Saturday afternoon at the cinema: a pirate had just dived from an immense height into the white stillness of ice-clear water. And I remember how it felt as if I had dived down with him. And I could still feel the water breaking open as my head passed beyond the surface, down into the blue silence of an altered world.

* * *

It was from childhood, long, long ago, and I was the one who saw it. It was the moment when death enters from the side door at the far end of the theatre, a lady in purple wraps, gossamer chiffon, trailing white smoke like a refrigerator exploding in a mausoleum, and the audience still neatly unwrapping their bonbons, still discretely working their gums, faintly intrigued by the silence on the stage, by the sudden absence of light. Lady Death in her make-up and the long white arm that reached out of the purple gauze. And on one side of me an elderly woman woke from her nap and, leaning across in the darkness where no one could see, whispered, "I have seen the handmaiden."

*   *   *

I read this once in a book and copied it down. I do not know
what book it was and have never found it again. I have always
wanted to read it to someone but never found the right person:

"If there is a light somewhere in the world it is not our light.
Whatever comes to us seems external. Hammerblows come
to us like light. However familiar they feel when they first hit
us, once they have come they are always unimaginable. Is this
the most we can ask of light? To squirm there on the floor,
beaten by the immense cattleprods of the divinity."

GASTON BOUSQUIN
(1957 – 2014)

GASTON BOUSQUIN: A PERSONAL ACCOUNT

From the moment I began the Ghostspeakings project –
setting down the translations, framing them with biographies,
interviews, personal accounts – I knew that sometime or
other I would have to write about my friendship with Gaston.
I would have to confront the difficulties of his life and my
own inadequacies. I have always been afraid of Gaston: he
is, he was, so much taller than me, stronger and with the
impulsive belligerence of a street-kid ageing slowly, almost
imperceptibly, into a pale flabby giant. In whatever apartment,
run-down hovel or luxurious borrowed houseboat I visited
him he would loom above me, threatening at any moment
to crush me in a hug or equally, offended by something said
or not said, slip a knife from a drawer and lunge with it at
my stomach. Then laugh when he saw my terror as the blade
retracted: it was a fake knife, you knew I was acting. But with
Gaston it was always real.

I will start with the early background, much of which
I only learnt later from his sister. As a teenager he left the
family home in a small town outside Montréal. His father
died when he was fifteen and there were always tensions
and explosions with his mother. Up to a point he modelled
himself on his uncle René, a constant traveller and dreamer of
big projects that always fell through, but Gaston's obsession
with poetry took him in a different direction. After spending
time in Montréal and British Columbia he decided that the
problem wasn't just his mother's home or Québec province

but the whole of Canada and the United States. He liked to say he was "allergic to the idea of north" and undertook his journey to South America to meet the true poets. (He had a love-hate relationship with his own language: "How much snow, how many fallen leaves can a poem take?" he would ask and then add, embellishing a conversation he had many times with me, "Beauty, that is the curse of French – you are lucky, you have an ugly language.") In Argentina he invited himself to Olga Orozco's house and also got to meet Osvaldo Lamborghini; in Uruguay he visited Marosa di Giorgio but generally failed to impress the local poets who considered him an ill-mannered clown. He worked hard at his Portuguese as well as his Spanish and spent some nine months in Brazil, teaching English and French, both of which he was perfectly fluent in, though he rarely wrote in English and didn't trust his ability to translate his own poems. He got to know Ricardo Xavier Bousoño and admired Wilson Bueno's work, but they never got on well. From what his sister said, I think at this time he was trying to invent himself. He had a knack of offending people but he could equally be extraordinarily generous and considerate. Though he spent most of his time in Argentina, Uruguay and Brazil, he also made short visits to Medellin, Caracas, Nicaragua and Mexico, as an invited guest at various poetry festivals. It was in Nicaragua that he met the Belgian poet William Cliff whose book *America*, along with its sequel *En Orient*, became a Bible to him for many years, so Gaston told me. (Personally, apart from the one poem in homage, I can't see any resemblance between Gaston's poetry and Cliff's.)

About three years later he returned very ill, broken, in some deep wordless depression. His sister took care of him in the family home; his mother, in a rigid state of denial, moved about the house. (Strangely, in the few poems that mention her, he always seems very positive about her.) His recovery was in fact quite quick and over the next five years he produced six books of poetry, published with various small presses in Québec. At that time he moved to Vancouver Island where he lived with various girlfriends, most of all Marie Johnson, whose partner he was, off and on, for the next ten years. He was still with Marie when they crossed the Pacific by yacht to Hawaii, then by plane to American Samoa and from there by ferries and slow boats to New Zealand. From Auckland they flew to Sydney, arriving in March 1997.

I met Gaston for the first time at a book launch in Glebe, perhaps in August that year. Exuberant, filled with enthusiasm and energy, he gave me the impression (I think this is how it was for many people) that through him there was a unique access to the intensity that poetry truly was and that, for all the time you were talking with him, he held you in the immense arms of his undivided care. We spoke for hours of poetry, of his travels. The three of us – Gaston, Marie and myself – stayed on till after midnight at a café, then met again many times over the following months till work and family pressures on my part forced me to live a far more anti-social life. It would have been about a year later that I visited him on the houseboat on Middle Harbour where he was staying. By that time he had broken up with Marie and was on his own. I can still remember the sound of the oars against the water as he rowed me across in the darkness to the squat brown frame of the house that lifted and fell on the waves. *"Nuit en moi, nuit au dehors,/ Elles risquent leurs étoiles,/ Les mêlant sans le savoir,"* he recited from Jules Supervielle, then continued, *"Et je fais force de rames/ Entre ces nuits coutumières."*[6] That night we spoke French all evening as he regaled me with stories of the poets he'd met, chiefly the amazing *bruja* Olga Orozco in her Buenos Aires apartment, still with the radiance of a powerful glamour in her sixty-year-old eyes, her elegant kaftan, her entourage of cats, her ability to see the future (inherited from her Irish grandmother, María Laureana), telling Gaston he would live one day on a houseboat somewhere in the far south of the world and that, when he died, it would be a terrible death that would send "ripples of warning" to many people. He also spoke of his friend Ricardo Xavier Bousoño whom he urged me to contact and to start translating. ("He is a great poet; not many people know about him," he told me. "I'm sure you could translate him well.") The houseboat was quite an extraordinary place, the one large living room all lined with books, a tiny kitchenette, a bunk bed in a kind of fold-out attic, the spacious bedroom downstairs. When I left he insisted on my borrowing many books: Supervielle, Reverdy, Jean Frémon, Tahar Bekri, Vénus Khoury-Ghata and Hédi Kaddour, among others. Only later did I discover that none of the books were his – they all belonged to the owners of the houseboat he was minding, Dominique and her partner Ariana who were away overseas on a sabbatical. (To my chagrin the elegant white cover of Frémont's *La Vraie Nature des ombres* was soon stained by a dark growing rim of coffee, while Reverdy's *Sources du vent* had disintegrated into a pile

6 "Night within me, night without/They risk their stars/Unconsciously mixing them/And I row strongly/Between these customary nights."

of winnowing pages. Should I confess it? – yes, I'll confess it – I still have their copy of Yves Bonnefoy's *Récits en rêve*.)

It was to be almost eight months before I met Gaston again. The change in him this time was dramatic: he looked decidedly aged and clearly had a drinking problem, something never evident before. He had a new girlfriend, Eleni, who seemed to share the same appetite for alcohol as himself and with whom he seemed to be having constant fights. At one of these meetings he presented me with a large envelope filled with a selection of his poems that he asked me to translate. These were all, I believe, fairly recent poems, written mostly while he was in Australia – the poem to Olga Orozco was, I'm fairly sure, written on the houseboat. It is mostly these poems that I have translated here, though there are also a few earlier ones and four very late ones, given to me after his death by his sister, Isabelle. Some of these final poems – "Robert", "Kim Le" and "Ahmed" – presumably come from his volunteer work in a young writers project in Bankstown. These last poems Isabelle gave me about two months after the funeral, after she began to realise she would never get a human response from people high up, people whose business was silence. So the order of the poems is not in any strict sense the chronological order of composition, though, overall, it may be close to the order of their biographical references. (There is also the curious poem "De celui qui luit", written long ago in Québec during his Michel Deguy phase, as he put it, in the French original and in his own quite aberrant English version, a separate poem, in fact. In this case I decided to include all three: his French original, his "translation", and my own translation of the original French.)

Gaston and I met fairly frequently over the following year and then, quite suddenly, I learnt he had returned to Canada. I received three letters from him in the next two years and, as I began work on the translations, corresponded via email. He seemed settled and calm, with a steady teaching job and a new relationship. There was talk of marriage and news of a book of micro-fictions. Then in 2008 I heard through friends that he was back in Sydney. I visited him in his place in Cremorne. We'd already met many times in the city, in Glebe and Newtown, but he wanted me to meet his new girlfriend Gisèle. The address he'd given me turned out to be in a high-rise block opposite the dentist I'd gone to as a teenager and in my early twenties. When I parked my car in an empty spot at the dentist's front door I could almost feel a throb of pain in my jaw.

When I reached the correct room on the eighth floor the door was ajar with a small post-it note stuck to it: "Come in – back in ten minutes." I went inside. Everything was in chaos. I sat down and waited, thinking of the strangeness of this place, of where he'd chosen to live: so far from where he worked, a private girls' school outside Penrith. He had no car. It would have to be a good two hours commute by public transport. I knew Sydney's public transport system: a mere fifteen-minute drive would often be an hour by buses: a city, like the country, committed to destroying itself. Gaston would be what, sixty by now, a little younger than me. On the table was a bundle of papers. One stuck out and, without really meaning to, I read it:

> *I may be completely impotent but I still have much to offer. I'm well endowed and I know certain tricks and I'm not a day over seventy.*

Blushing, I looked away. Was this a letter or part of a novel and why was it in English? I heard a noise from the interior of the flat like someone was moving around: the sound of someone falling out of bed, the shelf of a wardrobe collapsing maybe. Some more sounds. A girl in a bathrobe came out, maybe nineteen, maybe twenty-seven, blonde, wafer-thin like a model. She didn't see me, went to the sink, poured a glass of water, drank it, then turning noticed me and said in a decidedly French accent "You are Peter, right?", and without waiting for an answer went back into the bedroom. I could hear more sounds of disruption, then a shower being turned on.

Gaston arrived at the door, obviously drunk. His face was scarlet, his gestures excessive. Cradled in his arms were four bottles of wine. He reeked of some inexplicable kind of human decay. He made it across to the sink where he laid the bottles down one by one on their side.

He went into the bedroom: loud voices in French. I got up to leave but felt I had to at least say goodbye. Then Gaston came out and, seeing me standing up, said, "No, no, please stay. It's nothing, it's nothing. You've come so far. You must stay. Have a drink, we will eat." Then he went back into the bedroom. Sounds of a conversation shifting from heated to placatory. Now Gisèle came out again. "I must apologise. I have to go out for work but stay with him, please. He is in a bad space now," she whispered. "I know how much your friendship means to him. Stay with him, please," she whispered again, brushing my shoulder lightly with her hand. It was her touch that sealed it: that I should come that close, even for a moment, to her youthful presence. After she left, Gaston poured us both two ample glasses of wine and pulled two frozen fish fillets out of the fridge to cook. It seemed all there was to eat in that chaotic house. In his current alcoholic state I wouldn't have dared suggest a restaurant. The conversation slipped from this to that topic, but everything felt forced, difficult, like a perpetual evasion. We spoke a little of poetry, of his job, of his projects, of the state of the country and the world, but all in a circling maze of alcohol that made it impossible for me to keep up with his logic. When it seemed I had stayed more than long enough I left.

We met again: here, there, at literary events over the following years. I seemed to be making little progress with my translations. Then, early in 2014, came a phone call. It was Miguel. Had I seen the news? I have no television so, as we spoke, I turned on the computer and found the story:

> 62 year old Canadian citizen and Australian permanent resident dies in Villawood Detention Centre after being repeatedly tasered by security staff. The man was allegedly tasered nine times by three guards after raising his voice requesting a lawyer. How and why the man came to be locked up in the Detention Centre is unclear.

It was Gaston. In the following days the story emerged. Gaston had been visiting a group of friends, one of whom was a German tourist who had overstayed his visa. Because Gaston didn't drive he had no driver's licence or other form of ID on him and the immigration officials refused to believe his explanation that, as a permanent resident, he was here legally.

They bundled him and the German off to Villawood. When Gaston tried to phone people the three numbers he called all failed to pick up. After that, the battery on his mobile died. Two days later, when nothing seemed to be happening, Gaston approached a guard, demanding to see a lawyer. That was when they tasered him. The film footage smuggled out on another detainee's mobile showed it clearly. All Gaston did was raise his voice and be a tall man: it was enough to get him killed. The warning they gave was barely seconds before the tasering started and, once one guard began, two others joined in. The news report spoke of nine shots: I counted at least seventeen. After the fourth shot Gaston collapsed onto the ground. By the tenth shot he had stopped moving but they just kept firing.

GASTON BOUSQUIN (1957– 2014)
A SELECTED ANTHOLOGY

GASTON BOUSQUIN VISITS OLGA OROZCO IN HER BUENOS AIRES APARTMENT, LATE SUMMER 1981

She eyes the aquarium with its one remaining fish
and intones in the voice of the cat: "*Tú reinaste en Bubastis.*"
She goes under the water of her tiny aquarium
and hides there, goby-like, under the greyest rock.
She is invisible, knitted into
the long caul of her days.
When she returns, full-woman-size, through the front door
she takes a thin slip of paper
from a box of dreams by the broom closet
and watches the green and purple twists of smoke
rising from its pyre. In the crook of her arm,
on the white tips of her fingers,
lie traces of that shimmering light
things bring with them from the time
they first moved out of water. Exiles in the strange land
of carbon and air. She is a deity
of the other world. Through the sunken
eye of a rock-face, down the spiral of chiselled
steps she precedes me, the taut sway
of her African kaftan grazing the stone,
into the tropic garden of my future.
I am destined always
to misunderstand her, to
misrepresent her, to be a small carrier

of her transmuted inoperable virus.
She reincarnates and is born backwards
among her Irish and Italian ancestors.
Even perched on this sumptuous chair,
she feels puncturing her face
the stones that will lie above her grave.
Though I am talking to her in my halting Spanish
I already feel her presence
in the houseboat I will rent on Middle Harbour
and her smile, her shyness is there
waiting like a second shadow to greet me
beside the gruff Immigration Officer
at Friday Harbor. She is present
in the cigar that stuns me and weaves
circles of trance in my expensively imported head.
I walk out onto a balcony over a gully
and she is sitting there, nursing a cat –
it finds the hidden milk behind her long-dry nipple.
I sit in the chair opposite.
Neither of us can find words.
We both know what it is to come from the moon.
"Continue walking," she says to me without speaking.
"It is your destiny to walk to Patagonia.
Once you reach its final rocks you must pledge
always to stay south of the Equator.
You are not destined to find any home –
settling anywhere would prematurely tilt
the balance of your cerebellum into some
wayward dash into death.
Never trust the algorithms. Place yourself securely

in the isolated helm of going under.
Keep your eyes fully open
as the vampire insects of the cosmos swarm towards you.
Trust this solitude and what it says to you,
this reticent tongue-tied intelligence
that moves only in singularities.
Gleaned from what is much older than human,
recite the authentic contours of falling.
And now to cross this bridge of arsenic, as we say.

"Choose
but don't cheat, don't whisper any counter-spell,
any words of return."

THE MASS OF THE WEST WIND

for William Cliff

glory to those who dwell
in the silences of the world
in the hull of the tramp steamer
in the cargo freighter's oil and rust, the narrow cabin
hole in the wall of darkness
this bitter unglorified monastic cell
afloat in an ocean with no gods

glory to those who have rested in honesty
in the places where there is nothing
where evil has shaped its sharp
enduring scar –
lifeless avenues, spectral streets,
bars where no one risks crying or touching
or speaking anymore

glory to those who persist
in places where there are no words no images
no consolatory swirls of rhetoric
where to stay for five days
is to know the circle Dante
was too frightened to describe

glory to those who impose on the world
only the openness of their eyes
their truth

to each face of suffering
their tiny drained
willingness to be there

RESTAURANT ON STILTS, ORINOCO RIVER, AUGUST 1985

Underneath,
suddenly black water
wavers – a flash of primal dark between
the trembling planks of the restaurant.
Between one step and the next I stop
frozen: at once I know a whole continent
is draining by underneath me.
Mudflats and icefloes, badlands, urban waste,
all the forest's soft-bellied creatures,
the teeming eyes of the drowned, all rush
helter-skelter under these planks where
I freeze, hoping some stray lone hand
won't pull me under.
In whose flesh am I standing?
The prawn soup that is lunch trembles
six feet away but here, suddenly,
an arm's length from me is a space
I'll never cross.

In the whirling vortex of the world
all movement hushed:
the pouring of the dark.

INTERMEZZI

in the plane's dawn window
a book catches light

*

"trash, trash":
the singing voice of an angel
down the plane's cabin

*

in the slow blaze of wheat fields
two palm trees earn the trembling
slight displacement of prayer

*

isolated wind gusts incite the bougainvillea
to mime their alphabet:
florid red lips speaking silence

*

a family of lorikeets shiver in autumn wind:
the faint ringing of an immense church
made by these knotted boughs
that fail to touch

*

a small finger already broken from its green body:
the jasmine's first petal
offers itself to the air

*

among all the codices between earth and sky
the tiny one bearing the signature of my death

*

quiet night –
the guard asleep with his heavy holster,
at the house entrance the iron grille:
its bars glistening like a fountain of neon

*

burnt-out landscape of white houses,
black jagged trees, the odd
orange-blistered roof:
a cold air comes from the cold world

*

this lake is not a lake:
wound in the city's open hand:
a drowned mouth

*

Lightning flash burying itself
in the back of my eyes:

as if I had stepped through the large clumsy sky
to hold, all at once,
my birth and my death

WITH MARIE ON THE ISLAND

Like the carved prow of a boat
riding high above the waves
the house's front door opens wide onto the sea.
Kwakiutl lands.
My dark-haired beloved, thin and tall
like a weather-beacon against plummeting skies.
On a night of intermittent rain
we look out on the great quiet of small places:
under the single streetlight
a young girl in a polka-dot dress
blowing bubbles in the rain.

Eros has led me out into this garden of the world:
showers of rainbows in a sky of white stars.
Looking upward
she teaches me the names,
all the lore of the skyfolk
who move steadily across the heavens
over our garden.

HALLOWEEN AT FRIDAY HARBOR

1.

Ghosts and witches, bugs and tinmen,
all stroll down Main Street in the late
fall glow. Somewhere in the air above them
float other masks: wolf, raven, bear,
the boy who stole the sun.

Think twice if you are summoned
to the old house beyond the hill,
that wooden slab carved
with the open mouth of ancestry.
Consider carefully when you hear
a jagged edge to the afternoon breeze,
whistling from a mask that
gathers blood and must be broken,
a sound echoing in the hollows
of unknown wood

while around you a voice intones:

I am the canoe bundled with my bones
out of which trees bloom.
I am dizziness at the centre of light
and a cold breeze that has caressed
all earthly darkness.
When I close my eyes

I see the water circling
and the cold fish finding stillness.

2.

When I close my eyes
you are walking in strange costume
down hallways.
The feather in your hair, so
innocently smooth, is from
the bird that eats only eyes
while your frail brown
half-nakedness moves forward
under the command
of no force either of us
understands: a bell
is ringing always in my head
but it is not time or any
human season it measures.
In this place the sun and moon
are small disks that have been woven back
into the carpet.

Your feet are so sturdy
I would almost believe this planet
respects them. Almost.

TO ALEJANDRA PIZARNIK

I have been troubled for days by the dream I had of you, your face seen so clearly, your thin thirty-year-old self occupying a flat on a corner of George Street, Sydney. I do not know what to make of your insistent beauty, the art works I glimpsed in corners of your room, and your brusque persistence in smoking while the first-storey window misted over with the chill dawn off the southern ocean. I could go into the city right now and find you but I'm frightened of what your eyes would see in me, so little, and your confident knowledge of how to write beyond your death. In my dream I was going from entrance to entrance in the hope of finding the poem you left for me. The first entrance was a bricked-up wall like those false doorways masons built to hide the maze that descends towards the Queen's Chamber of a pyramid. The second an open bar that had run out of drinks where the stairways and landings of three floors fed back into themselves like an Escher print of a Moebius tube. Only, above the fake third door, a rope ladder dangled to take me to your studio. I didn't dare climb up. You were wearing a beret when you leaned out to drop something, an eagle's feather, a plastic earring. I'm guessing even now at how little I mean, jostled by the throng of New York twenty-something party girls in miniskirts, all so blasé about sharing their building with the starlets of film, fashion and literature. And what do they or I know of what it costs to persist despite illness and death? I can't explain why this dream has lingered under all my waking thoughts for over a week now. Maybe I had been summoned there to play some bit part in the vast saga you were writing of interplanetary grief. Maybe the feather and bauble were meant for me after all, hungering always for the lightning flash of poetry, arriving at your apartment, Montevideo 980, ten years after you'd gone for good.

AT SEVENTY-NINE UNCLE RENÉ RECOUNTS HIS LIST OF BLESSINGS

That the sun rises

That the colour blue has occurred in more than one place in my world

That I have known oceans, slipped into them, been stung into life by their unexpected surges

That light has gathered around me in mist-wrapped valleys under dank trees, that the spiders have continued untroubled connecting the threads of light

That water persists in falling, from clouds to earth, from high escarpment to sudden gully, to the tug of subterranean streams, to pools that gather their crystalline essence of sky, to the steady drift towards deltas, to collapsed citadels, the vast inverted mansions of darkness

That I have entered water, have dreamed my way under its shelter, have stood inside the waterfall, been gripped by it

That stars have listened, just by being there have listened, in ways I can't understand, ways trivial and profound, have heard my voice and other voices, all night have heard seas building and collapsing, have heard burrowers and possums and every nocturnal creature attending to the scratched hum of their own silence

That the stars have lasted and are still there, listening like the grandmother of all grandmothers watching over the generations, nodding, then turning aside, gone back to some endless routine of renewing the fires of the cosmos

That fish are still here despite everything, despite the millennia of killing, the centuries of poisoning, that they investigate, dart off, breathe fire through their bodies

That houses are still inside me, that I can recite the location of cupboards and fireplaces, can look out a back window and number the chinks in each rock, that I still hold the thread of their labyrinths

That I have stood in the narrow room, have been that close to the glittering living statue, the Eternal Couple, he always erect and inside her, she straddling him, her legs holding him firm, the lovers who sustain the world

DE CELUI QUI LUIT

De celui qui luit
les yeux deviennent on dit
l'éclairage de cette digue
sombre faîte des rocailles
du coeur noirâtre de ce monde
celui qui
autrefois
restait là
baigné de soleil
dans l'espace d'intervalle
entre les deux rivages
le passé et ce terrain de camping où les femmes l'attendent
leurs visages lui offrant le bonheur du soleil

maintenant
la torche dans sa main devenue sa main
devenue lui-même qui
reste debout là
dans cette nuit au coeur du monde
c'est à lui d'être la lumière
condamnée
à luire
à lire ce qui reste

OF HE WHO LIGHTS THE CAUSEWAY

Of he who lights
the causeway
charcoal boulders, granite slabs
patch of soil where once
he sunned himself
one afternoon
rested sunned and single
with his notebook
skies and shores before him
in light the sun gave to him then

his hand now lights
the torch become his hand
become himself
light beacon
on the path between two shores
black waves all round
all faltering all falling
at the world's black core
himself self-reader
condemned
to be light

(translation by the author: Gaston Bousquin)

OF THE ONE WHO SHEDS LIGHT

Of the one who sheds light
his eyes they say
light up this causeway of rough stones
of this world's blackened heart
some time back
he'd be there always
bathing in sun
in the space that lies
between two shores:
the past and this camping ground
where the women are waiting,
their faces offering him
the sun's happiness.

For now
the torch in his hand
has become his hand,
become himself
standing there
in this night at the world's heart:
it's up to him now to be the light
condemned to shed light
the reader
of what's left.

(*translation of the original French by Peter Boyle*)

HE TRAVELS INTO HIS LANDSCAPE

They surround him in his wheeled chair, some of them guiding, some pushing, others simply walking on one side or the other. Collapsed and battered, clothes awry, only half aware of what's happening, he follows his body from somewhere slightly above it. At the riverbank they manoeuvre the wheeled contraption onto a raft, then push the raft away from shore while, onboard, two young boys take charge of paddling.

They have barely made it away from the riverbank, have just entered the swirl of the main current when the raft starts sinking. Layers of water lap in over the deck. Soon the whole wooden structure is going under as the two boys, unable to swim, frantically go on paddling. Then, in one moment, the raft plummets. His contraption too is sinking but his body, slipping relaxed out of its seat, floats. Half in, half out of consciousness, he floats.

Hours pass, a night passes and he has drifted far downstream. Two girls are playing in the water. His hearing gone, he recognises them at first from the fragrance in the water – it enters his mouth, his nostrils, a rich fragrance of blossoms, of unstoppable life. They are naked apart from a wrapping of leaves at their waist, two dark-skinned girls from the lower reaches of the river – the great river that rises in Asia and slowly drops down into Africa.

The girls find a wide hoop made of knotted vines and pass this over his body. Three times they slowly circumscribe his body with the hoop – at no point does he stir, at no point recognise them. They would like to perform some magic on him, to cut some morsel of his flesh, mix it with herbs and spells, and make him young again but know this can't really be done. Using the hoop they simply steer his body to shore, careful at all times not to touch it. Then they leave.

It is night again. In the darkness a glow like a cluster of intense fireflies hovers over him. It is the five judges, visible only as a faint light in the air. He perceives their stillness and their whispering. He can hear the chanting that goes on under their paper crowns, their garments of shredded air. He does not expect justice or mercy. It is only so that every ritual may happen, that a door in the sky may open. He fears fire, but if there are only worms? He wishes he had kept the scrolls that had been left to him in the bottom drawer of the desk. He could have had a garment made of them, could have worn the insignia of life and death, then the judges might read the scrolls and organize for the door in the sky to be opened. But now he is left this side of the tribunal with only the markings on his hand for them to read, for them to make sense of. On this side, he understands now, there is only earth and water, only worms and the persistent curiosity of lizards.

At that moment he sees himself alone and naked, seated in a small antique chair. Beside it, the cane chair of his mother, empty as it has been for so long. And around him, a thousand, thousand books from the library of madness.

WINTER MORNING

At the hour when wolves become dogs and dogs become wolves
a fox crossed my path.
Postal deliverer or inspector of houses
he halted to nod vaguely
in my direction.
On the tapestry of thin spiky grass
a princess has wept, leaving
an embroidery of small purple flowers.
The fox continues joyfully on
to some imagined spot where
a loose run of chickens meets
the high-wire loops of dangling lost ends.
The fox will not hang himself for love of the princess.
She has gone and is now only these flowers.
I pick them to make
a bouquet for the absent one,
the beautiful young girl who is always
arriving and departing,
whose forehead has now
left a dint in my forehead while I slept.
The latch of the side-gate clicks in a puff of air
behind her as she exits
down the path to the river
and the wide ravenous mornings of the world.

In the sink now gathering mould,
in the six months since her death,

the long rim of a bowl has trapped
a fox chasing a princess chasing a fox.

ROBERT

After the cancer
after the divorce
after the retrenchment
he moved the stones one by one in the garden.

KIM LE

A tree turns its white stillness
like a mourning woman
three a.m.
her nudity for no one.

From the strange mildness of her face
she gazes outwards:
neighbours' fences,
all the past behind them.
She knows the statue of the Buddha sits
in many a cruel house,
the fingers of bitterness counting
hoarded notes.

But at midday here she is
planting seedlings in the chill garden,
basil, onion and garlic
and the mint she will stir against the broth
as the thinly sliced meat
cooks itself in water.

AHMED

Rocking awkward in the small chair
like a giant stranded in a doll's house,
each day he comes to class to be retrained,
this young man who might be fifteen, might be twenty four.
"I sit for five minutes, then I have to stand
and move about, or my fists
keep feeling like they have to punch out hard –
that's how it's always been:
why am I like that?"
On his head his baseball cap
sits neither forwards nor backwards
but tilted sideways.
His innocence steps out cautiously to gaze around
while on the desk his hands
all by themselves arrange and rearrange
pens, a mobile phone, some crisps for lunch,
a folder of lined pages.
"My parents want me to go to Uni,
be a doctor or lawyer, join the police force,
shit like that –
just normal things like other parents.
So why does everybody hate us?"
And day after day he comes back
to tilt again at this bizarre tournament
of words and numbers.

Despite everything he's there again
each five minutes at the desk
writing the world.

EVENING, SCOTLAND ISLAND

On inward-tilted hills
a still shadow.
Sky wide bats glide down darkened air.
Out there the last caw, last
jittery shudder of a bough.
Look – from circle to circle
now the inner glow of things.

PACKAGE RECEIVED FROM MEXICO CITY, DECEMBER 2015

TRANSLATOR'S NOTE

I was about to send the manuscript of *Ghostspeaking* to the publisher when a package arrived at my door. It was late December 2015, my commitments to various projects well overdue, when the front-door bell sounded and I opened to find a postal employee with an express delivery item. So I signed the key-pad and accepted a small package post-marked Mexico City. (Interestingly, the addressee's name on the documentation was "Doyle" but the young man who delivered didn't seem to notice the discrepancy.) The package came from a friend of a friend, Chus Ramirez, owner of *Tronos y Dominios*, a bookshop on Calle de Caracoles Invisibles in the San Angel district. He knew of my interest in Maria Zafarelli Strega and, now that this package had reached him, decided to make a copy and send it on to me, along with a photo of Maria as a young woman posing for a solo shot just before the presentation of the Rio Plate Anthology. In a short note he explained how a friend of his, Victor Schlossky, a small-time arms dealer and amateur financier of poetic enterprises, had forwarded it to him to examine the writings and, if he wished, have them published or otherwise disseminated. Maria Zafarelli Strega, a friend of Victor's, had sent the package to him a few weeks before. It may well be one of the last things she posted to anyone. Her body was found, emaciated and riddled with poison (apparently self-administered) in a small house on the edge of a town in the Sonora Desert. She had been living in Mexico for three years under the name Isabel Avellaneda Moncloa. Chus's letter, so plain and factual, left me stunned and confused. I could not accept the news of her death. Suddenly I realised how much I had always expected her to outlive me.

The package contained high-quality photocopies of nineteen handwritten pages but ten of these pages, the ten central pages, consist of the one sentence written over and over: *Cada palabra abre un cadáver* (Every word opens a corpse). I have decided to replace the ten pages with ten lines. The remaining pages on either side I have translated faithfully. What I cannot reproduce is the exquisite eloquence of Maria's handwriting. It is small, sometimes vanishing to a sinuous curve at the end of words, especially with verbs, where the slight rise of the letter "b" alone indicates that this is one form or another of the continuous past (also called, as if everything couldn't be described this way, the imperfect). The loops of the b's, l's and o's stake their claim on elegance while other letters, like "f" and "t", vary constantly in how they are written, sometimes timid, sometimes exuberant like wind-beaten signposts defying the white desert all around them. The name VICTOR is written entirely in capitals with small thorn-like tendrils winding above and below them. Often letters are not joined to each other. Repeatedly with different forms of the verb "to be" – *está, están, estamos, estaba* and so on - the separate syllables of the word are split and seem to be heading off in different directions. And yet the overall impression is of great decisiveness, deliberation and firm control. The careful balance between white space and script, the shifting dialogue between a stark plainness and wildly elaborating curves, give the sense that she was working her way towards some new, yet-to-be-revealed aesthetic. It is the writing of someone who values their own writing and who, whatever they may be saying, believes in the survival of beauty.

The photo is a cameo shot in black and white, set against a deliberately blackened background. Her hand rests on her right cheek. There is a ring, a plain band, on the fourth finger. Shadows play across the centre of her face and her hair, which is short, falls across the left side of her face. Her gaze is sideways on but she doesn't seem to be looking at anything. The photo appears as if it could have been taken in the mid 1960s but it was shot by Antonio Beynton on August 15, 1993. I think, as a still very young recently discovered poet, she wanted to give the impression of intense focus, seriousness and profundity. What I see is walls closing in all around and the determination, somewhere in the space behind the eyes, that, beyond sadness, there is a world to be created. Yet if I look for long at the photo I find it unbearable. I start to feel myself sinking with her, drawn into the magnetic pull of a silence without end.

PACKAGE FROM MEXICO CITY

We are all dead now. I am the trace left by a spider's progeny caught in a whirlwind that glides haphazard over the desert mesa.

The mesa is writing itself. In my dream of androgyny my shaven head is the bare ouija board of the badlands.

*

Little squiggles appear in the night sky to tell me
you can't do it tomorrow
because there is no tomorrow.

*

Victor lifts me out of my madness and rebirths me, like a tired sick car, in the desert of Sonora.

He says, We can't rid you of your silvery Argentine accent but we can rebadge you as someone here for a shamanic cure. All your papers will show you as Isabel Avellaneda Moncloa, IAM.

IAM = now (Latin) = I AM (English) = confiture compressed
                              out of clotted endings, clutched
                              straws, berries in a mincer, herbage
                              of a home unhealed unhearthed

IAM = jambe cut short   leg unlengthened
    un-*jota*'d Jaime robbed of his inner i lamenting
    io io on   the steps of
    the monument   poor cow led to the slaughter

IAM = Ishtar (Maria)   Alpha (Z)   La Maga (Strega)

*

sitting on a stairway removing the stones of time

a mole underground   a midge in water   a mite in air

making its moon-ward way
meanderer of punchdrunk miles

*

– What is it that you want from me?
There he was, the small man with dark imp-like features, a
dwarf suddenly there in a corner of the room. The door was
closed and I was sure he had not entered that way. He seemed
to have come up through the floorboards though there was no
gap visible to indicate his passage.
    Although I had never met him I knew who he was.
He addressed me again.
    – You prowled your way through my work all those years
ago when you were sixteen before you'd even left school. You

wanted to learn my language, to look underneath every word I'd left. And you hadn't even started your own life. Now here you are again – prowling through my books all over again. Only this time you're on the edge of leaving this world altogether and, who knows, maybe everything is behind you now. So I'm asking: what is it you want of me?

And I am floored by this imp. I don't know what I want of him, of others like him, what I expect any writing or painting or music to give me, what I expected it to do all those years ago in the face of life, what I expect of it now facing my own death.

And just as suddenly he is gone. The room is empty. There is no sulphurous smell of the devil though I am sure he came from the underworld. And I ask myself: what can anyone give another when one's own words can't answer before life or death? I wondered suddenly if what he had been saying in his books all along was simply that everything is unprecedented – so we must always be wandering astray, always heading off in the wrong direction since we can't know our own direction and if we don't need to start at all we shouldn't, and if we have started because it seemed necessary we must stay with the difficulty.

And now that he had gone I became aware of the river flowing powerfully through my bedroom. It had no water and was not visible in any way, but there was a clear sense of a vast flood streaming through the room so that I had to stay huddled on the bed so as not to be swept away by it. And, as I watched its energy tugging at everything in the room, I sensed it was a river that had started flowing with greater and greater strength now I had come here, living alone in this house that tottered and swayed around my small bed. And yet there were also visitors who slept in cages suspended here and there in corners of other rooms or in the hallway or the passage that led down some stairs to the out-house. Not that they were locked in their cages. They set the cages up themselves with rope ladders attached so they could pull them up when they felt the need for greater privacy or safety, to keep themselves secure from the other beings that came and went through the walls of the house at all hours – creatures that were certainly not exactly human but might be small and still bite or leave great wounds in the face or neck, or else substances that might be invisible but could insinuate their way into an eye or an ear while a person was sleeping. And there were also larger creatures, shadows that moved along walls or temporarily darkened windows, beings too big to fit into the house who swept past above it or below it, to one side or the other. Such was the place I now lived in.

*

death-planting   each one self-knotted
the voice of the cricket   the voice of the cicada
the moth and the maggot   whisper

"you have sliced the cosmos with your knife"

while the curve of the sky curls over
earth-tilt without end
magnificent splinters

fear wipes them   wipes their breath
off the slate of the world

*

Terrified after the death I'd wanted for so long, didn't plan,
had nothing to do with, but felt responsible for, since it
was exactly what I'd always dreamed of – and then nothing
solved, the past, the things so painstakingly suppressed, alive
the same as ever. Childhood, my teenage years. Things seen,
things heard. The hauntings, pills again and then, later, all
through my skull and spine a different pain. The disease with
the long name I choose not to say. Flying north for treatment.
Frightened of everyone, the living and the dead, I take on my
third name. My third self enters the sanatorium. Six months
later, broken, half-crazed, I fly north again, this time to
Mexico, under my fourth name. I am seeking the eternal, the
nameless, the most anyone has in the end, the cure by magic.

*

They go along the avenues, they climb the path under the
trees, between the rosebushes, their eyes dull indentations of
missing glasses that once read the furthest stars. And these
scooped caverns of blindness they offer me are half sorrow,
half the weight of all they have carried. Bent-double figures
trailing the familiar path, the taller one feeling her way with a
cane, the younger one clutching the taller woman's skirt. They
come from the most expensive shopping mall in the earth's

hidden underside, crowded with moles and thrifty rabbits and with ravens and inquisitive hoopoes flaunting crests and backs inscribed with the white-fire on black-fire prayers for the dead. And, as they approach me along the path, on the curving verge of forever, their faces are all pallor and infinite resilience.

I have seen baskets of cracked eggshells left at doorways. I have seen hands numbering the glass shards placed as offerings on the landing outside an old woman's bedroom. Poison and rest, rest and poison. And a small eye-dropper of unclouded vision. Gifts that come at such a high price. Only the most lost can afford them, those who wander the paths of the underworld with their baskets of broken treasure.

*

Old women I saw in my vision last night,
one tall, one short
bound by the cloaks that
match you, latch you and lock you,

bird women with hollows for eyes,
beaks twisted back
into convoluted, impossibly thin
musical instruments of long dried-out silence,

ignoring me,
fingering me, now down my gaunt grey
skin, now in my tangled insides,

rosy as old crushed curls of a dying bloom

you linger outside my window
you sing me
you come for me
and always, you come

*

cada palabra abre un cadáver
cada palabra abre un cadáver
cada palabra abre un cadáver
cada palabra abre un cadáver
cada palabra abre un cadáver
cada palabra abre un cadáver
cada palabra abre un cadáver
cada palabra abre un cadáver
cada palabra abre un cadáver
cada palabra abre un cadáver

(every word opens a corpse)

*

In my twenties I hungered so desperately for fame – admiration
for my poems, recognition as the one to watch, to take note
of. All that anxiety and elation when my thin book of poems,

printed for me by a friend with all its typos, appeared – and again the same a few years later when I was the star in the Rio Plate Anthology, giving my first and only interview for press and radio, the green talisman I wore under my dress for my readings, offers of publication for things I hadn't even written. Now it is anonymity I seek, the chance to become completely nameless, to vanish.

*

Recently I have started burning my notebooks. I read, copy out a few entries here and there onto some new pages, set those aside, then burn the original. I will send a few very small packages to Victor in Mexico City. The rest I will burn.

*

A purple and orange desert flower appeared overnight after the rain – there are small blue flowers and a field of gold buttons but only one of this flower I will call for now the Lady from the Devil's Antechamber. She is a handmaiden of darkness who needs great heat and only a sprinkling of rain to cross the frontier into this world. From the centre of her purple cup, orange stamens lift and writhe in the hot wind. When I come close to look ants are swarming through this exposed chalice and the purple leaves are corrugated tin sheets, hard and frightening to touch. In all the landscape visible from here she has chosen only one spot to appear. She has broken through the earth exactly where my left foot would rest when I move the chair and table outside to write in the cool of early morning. Perhaps she has taken it as her mission to grab me by the foot and drag me down to the underworld. I don't think so. But I'll not go too close either, and I'll offer her something so she won't punish me for my transgression.

*

During the night an immense strong wind lifted and shook the house for several hours. It circled and circled. Only my mother's wedding ring, there on the fourth finger of my right hand, kept it at bay.

*

I enter a shop down an alley in a part of the city I have never visited before. I look at a display of vast pelts of human skin, other bodies I might inhabit if I wish to continue, if there are still surgeons adept in the mysteries, if buying and selling remains a practice, if my currency holds out. And then I see it. I understand. The marks, the engravings on skin after skin. I keep tattooing myself on everything. The dark space around my eyes from my photo at age twenty-three, the intricate lines my hands held at thirty, they are all there, on these skins. And, when I thumb through a catalogue of available names in the folder that stands on the counter, the letters shimmer into variations of me. With no escape. And the woman who

343

sells the cure by magic says, "For you this is not available. You have used up your share of lives."

*

I sat next to you as you unfolded your papers, thin strips handled with such painstaking care, as if you were placing your entire life, all that would be left of you, into these repeated gestures of unfolding, licking, folding. As you did this, the intensity with which you spoke to yourself (or to these slips of paper) was art such as it might have been practised in temple dedications in Egypt five thousand years ago. Knotted like memory threads, like some yet-to-be-deciphered hereditary quipus, your consciously stilled, ochre-stained fingers hesitated, worked together, then hesitated. Did you write words on the small papers? Sometimes – notes to yourself or magic combinations of letters; mostly not, and then you licked, folded, set them aside and, when the sun was at its strongest, you took them to the sawn-off petrol drum on the back porch and burnt them. I did not intervene or ask. I watched you do it all: you my double, my enemy, myself.

*

Day by day the pains have been diminishing and I am writing more. I hope soon to fill the first of many packages to send to Victor who can organise their eventual publication. I may even resume my original chosen name, re-emerge as MZF.

*

The throbbing that comes out of the red glow of evening. A cloud of grey insects hovers around my head whenever I step outside or sit for a moment on the veranda. They gather there, glued to each other, like a shop-worn wedding garland tilted awry.

*

I have been stricken for a week now by extreme exhaustion and moments when time and space seem to shift about. The weekly trip to the nearby market town of Las Pedradas to buy food has become too difficult. The neighbours the other side of the barranca have agreed to prepare food for me and bring it over once a day. It was their suggestion. They seem all right though I often realise they are hiding something from me. Sometimes I wonder if their eyes, with that dull flicker of green moonlight, conceal bad intentions.

*

As I sleep I walk backwards across a bridge, down a lane, trying to retrace my steps. The shrapnel of fifty years breaks loose from some benign spot on my left shoulder and severs a leg or takes out an eye. A hand that is not mine but has hidden inside mine works its way down my body to bend one leg under me so I stand leaning on a wall for support, hoping the building won't decide to take a step back.

And, without understanding fully what it means, I hear myself pronounce the words: "You are everyone because you are no one."

*

It is the Day of the Dead and in the distance the night sky flares with fireworks. The next morning the couple from across the barranca comes with a plate of tortillas and a thick dark sauce, slightly greasy. The woman is tall, thin, spectral, with a shock of violent black hair; the man squat and heavy. With their hawk-like faces they assess and assess, assay and assay. I am pricked open. A taste of sharp metal enters me and my skin tingles. Lacking the energy to drive them off, slowly, compliantly, I eat.

*

You have assembled your tribe of ghosts who migrate with you. From country to country they have travelled with you. Now it remains to be asked: will they migrate with you when you cross over into the rock and clay, stone and earth realm of the gone forever?

*

I remember the day I left Buenos Aires – the dense, extraordinary rain. I dose myself slowly with the painkillers. And the knowledge somewhere inside me that I will never see any of this again.

*

Where there was nothing
night-etched fragrances now drift
a sudden awakening of the bamboo-lattice window
left open under a sinewy acacia's
rusted branches

The white spider ate death with its single black tentacle,
absorbing and absorbing, on the floor
where slabs of hot stone emit the sun's history
in a steady, quite audible throb
       And at the same time I feel its double, its living ghost,
climb my arm,
searching for the crumbling
white paper cup of the heart

*

roads that set out
crossing dusty tram-lined boulevards

skirting the intersecting grids
of wind-scoured trees,
dry bald slopes, thorn-bushes,
gorges studded in prickly pear,
to wind up at harbours, curves of chill ocean,
esplanades that climb above the sea

and, perched in its patch of blue sky,
my grandparents' house
where I am ten years old
leaning on the fence at the back
watching a liner vanish past the headland

RICARDO XAVIER BOUSOÑO
(ADDITIONAL TRANSLATION)

FINAL UNPUBLISHED MANUSCRIPT GIVEN TO TRANSLATOR

I had only seen the poem "Threads" in manuscript form on Bousoño's bundle of separate pages. The form, though unusual, was easy to grasp. In book layout, I suddenly realised, it becomes more difficult.

Think of a page as having three positions: the left margin (1), the centre (2), the right margin (3). A thread is hung in any one of these positions. The first thread starts in position one, the next in position two, etc. Once a thread has been hung it can only stay in the position where it has been suspended. So, for example, a thread in position three will stay in position three as we turn the page. If a thread is lucky some word in it will generate a new thread. For a while both threads continue to drop down the page together but soon the old one dies. The movement of reading is downward and slow, staying with the thread, and turning back the page where necessary to pick up a new thread that has appeared. In turn the new thread spawns another thread. We shift in order from position one to two to three, then back to one. Eventually the thread finds no word to trigger its continued life in another thread. Finis.

THREADS

Here
in the forest
clearing
where
names disappear
and the wailing
of revellers' songs
down laneways
at 4 a. m.
can no longer
keep the
ghosts at their
distance
all that clears
is blue light
a thinness
I've
never known
a silence more
foreign than
the furthest language
there is
no more
distance
to walk
emptiness
pours into me

transfixed by
nothing I can name
all the world
behind me
closes its
doors
If
I am
lifted up
I will enter
the air
Who is
guiding me
who is
almost at the edge
of speaking
sunlight
white

presence   presence
of   of
no matter   stone
no being   hard round
in   cold
one   guardian
line   where skinks
cleaves me   catch warmth
my past   where moisture
walks away   where
and is   memory
stillness   grows micro-

of
pure air

gardens of
inter-stellar
spores
long
fingers
the toadstools
leave
skat of
the first
invisible microbe
excreting
that
dank
moisture
we have
no name for
decomposition
of the cosmos
soft
transformed to
hard
transformed to
soft

soft
wisps
of grey-green
spittle
become
a
hand

lover
whose breast
I hold
in whose
body I
move and live
and afterwards

whose mouth
takes me
and
brings me
again
sky
beyond
the sky
while
a tap leaks
a siren
flares up
then moans
sullenly
for hours
unheeded
memory jolts   unheeded
as washing   in the din
gathers in   of death
the sink
soiled clothing
my other
life pouring
out between
the scrubbing
knuckles
voltage
in the pipes
and I see myself
(exile days

as under
other rooves)
at Atocha
the train
to the south
just left
seconds before
doors
closed now
like cells
inside me
taking their
own path
to head off
down
blind forking
corridors
some switch
within the
body's code
gone wrong
or in a Paris room
leaving at dawn
hunched
in each one's
private failure
against   against
a sky   or
of endings   in the name of
that now in   the Unspoken

the washbasin
become this
debt of
shit and blood

One
they erase
our being
a life's
bric-à-brac
china cups
flowers on
balconies
cupboards
crowded with
these small photos
gazing outward
bundled off
by hands in sterile
gloves
doors sealed the
evidence
removed
a quiet burning
like corners
folded back
crammed
in the incinerator
of all we were

these small photos
hunched
and swaying
at the piano
(another of
my tribe who
got away)
my lover
the pianist
clinging
against
invisible
hurricanes
as on the
raft of
his life
a plaited band of
string
at his wrist
his black

hair all
swirling
lost in
where he is
as I
will never be
the small
sharp light
of a makeshift
stage
an unknowable
attunement of
earth's chaos
drilling itself
into the wild
focus of
his fingers
a ghost's
presence
stepping inside
his
flesh
ek-stasis
his
way out
(for
each of us
burned into
memory
faces of those

into the white
blaze
of silence
these sounds
I utter
threads we
weave to lay
hold of
the past
the sounds
are
the last threads
holding things
after they have
vanished
after the
nameless ones
smash the china cups
shred the photos
empty
our apartments
and remove us
from
the list of beings
so that

we loved
prisoners
loaded on
planes tossed
like sacks
into the white
and frozen
ocean)

a moment ago
may not
altogether vanish
I enter the forest
where trees
soar over me
where I am lifted
among leaves
and I go down
the stairwell
of the syllables
criss-crossed
birds' speech
creak of branches
balancing me
mulch ticking
with spores
migrating
roots
burrowing
I enter the
darkness
which is not
silence
sounds
echoing off
the walls
of the world   of the world
                                  I come from
                                  under

small town rain
small town
terror
the streets
clogged with mud
the corner store
sprawling trees
gnawed at by
the sky
the square where
servant girls
trade stories
farmers' wives their
entourage of baggage
pools
of slime
after rain
second-best shoes
mud-stained
I'm walking still
among it
a whistle from
a doorway
and the quiet
vicious
intensity
of ordinary
deaths
chokes me
this evening

the twelfth day
of   of
searing heat   a certain
here in my   light
ninth floor flat   falling
Veracruz   all around
June 11   our silence
in the tenth year of   this island
the new   where I
dying   might have gone
millennium   the two
                            young operatives
                            the bullet
                            to the brains
                            the processing pit
                            that is
                            a faint grey
                            streak
                            across the
                            day
                            this morning as
                            I tilt the
                            phial
                            of morphine
                            balancing
                            the searing
                            fire
                            of pain
                            against
                            the extra hours

of being here
I write
script
of some
divine
(some joke)
chuckle
poor lebens
dolmetscher
or in a
kitchen where
whisked eggs
frothing
into omelette
laced with
sumac
and the ring
of a bowl
accidentally
tapping a
fry pan
are a lover's
tilted gaze
in
a rented room
far elsewhere
unbuckling
belts
all that
our fingers

between
each breath
the mind
descends
(the blurred
pain
all over me
fine nails
brushing fire
against the shell
that holds me)
I enter the
millwheel
and

found
of the breathless
gliding
at the level
of tin roofs
our view
across favelas
into this
momentary
stillness
of God
this
now
always
memory
instant
between
the (three
years now)
sharp
knife blades

clock-house of
the benevolent
spiders
from far off
I hear
voices
(tides of
anger
about to
break
over me)
a child before
my father's
downtown office door
the silver gleam
of its surface
where
trapped forever
I see
my awkwardness
this body
I couldn't
own or give
back
or in the
spider's inner
clock-house
I see myself
aged twenty-two
walking off the bridge

into Brazil
free and alive
a clean slate
for the decades
to inscribe
all the wild
colours
pouring through
the
third eye
in this still
space
between
two breaths
a
nowhere-bubble
bearing
all my life
crests of calm
this
emptying
out
this
momentary
ghost-becoming

a
nowhere-beacon
flares
behind
barred windows
glow
of two bodies
on rainy season
nights
a simple trust
that flares
beyond
the world
bright
tramcars
on steep streets

bells of
vendors' carts
beside a
church's
small
side entrance
poised women
strolling
on evenings when
a storm has
almost come
bright
flutter of kites
above a line
of housetops
avenues
that open to
the sea
bougainvillea blossoms
bangled wrists
and ankles
shimmering their
music
scents of
fried bananas and
dried fish
narrow doorways
children
huddling
while

a great rain
passes
I
hold fast
to what is

(Ricardo Xavier Bousoño: manuscript poem given to the translator, August 2010.)

ACKNOWLEDGEMENTS

Ghostspeaking is a work of fiction. The imaginary poets are composite characters and are not intended to represent, much less caricature, any individual poet. Like Proust's Vinteuil, Elstir or Bergotte, they each have aspects of several people to which I have added details from my imagination or from my own life. The poems and prose passages are not intended as pastiche or parody. My fictive poets do, however, bear traces of various poets and writers. Sometimes it is a trace of a poet's style, a favoured subject matter or a form for writing a poem. Sometimes it is more an attitude towards poetry. Occasionally it is an echo of some part of a poet's life. The reader will have already encountered in this book the names of many of those real poets so traced or "ghosted." There are others to whom I am indebted whose names have, so far, not appeared. Among them I would like to acknowledge respectfully Gastón Baquero, Gerardo Deniz and José Kozer.

The translations of the epigraphs from Alejandra Pizarnik and Marcel Proust at the front of the book are my own. In Ernesto Ray's "My lover's shoes (this morning)" the phrase "the shoes of wandering" is from Galway Kinnell's *The Book of Nightmares*. In the mysterious figure who meets Antonio Almeida one critical night in Montevideo and, with characteristic humility, does not wish to give his name, the reader may well detect the presence of the visionary teacher Chouchani, whose life is explored in Salomon Malka's *Monsieur Chouchani*.

I would like to thank Stuart Cooke and Aashish Kaul for their valuable feedback on an earlier draft of this book and Chris Andrews for his ongoing encouragement and support.

CPSIA information can be obtained at www.ICGtesting.com
Printed in the USA
LVOW11s1551201016

509596LV00005B/837/P